LAUGHLIN

Crown and Cross Book One

SKYLAR WEST

Published by Blushing Books
An Imprint of
ABCD Graphics and Design, Inc.
A Virginia Corporation
977 Seminole Trail #233
Charlottesville, VA 22901

Skylar West
Laughlin

eBook ISBN: 978-1-64563-939-8
Print ISBN: 978-1-64563-940-4
v1

Chapter 1

Suri

I gazed out to the sea, sighing in contentment, as I ground my feet gently into the forgiving sand, loving the feel of the gritty wetness. My nostrils flared at the robust and pungent blend of seaweed and salt emanating from the expanse of water. I surveyed my playground, my happy place, the sea.

As I stretched out my arms, the moonlight danced on my skin, catching me in its silvery embrace. I felt sexy and alive as the light danced on my body. I was hypnotized by the rolling waves cast in the light from the moon and stars overhead.

My journey had begun, like I assumed many others had, with an invitation. A co-worker invited me to join her at a yoga retreat. She sensed I was unhappy and wanted me to have a positive experience and meet her cool yogi crew in New York.

On a lunch break near the end of that transformational weekend, I was knocked out and kidnapped by my stalker husband. When I came to, I was tied to our bed back in our home in Boston. Edward became utterly unhinged, as he admitted to some pretty heinous crimes, including setting up a bevy of women at different locations around the country.

Edward admitted to millions of dollars in profits being skimmed from his father's company and a warrant out for his arrest. With the knowledge of his impending arrest. Edward lost it and planned on shooting me and then himself. I guess he decided he couldn't do time for his crime and couldn't stand the idea of being alone, even in death.

Edward had been spotted dragging my unconscious body into his vehicle by one of my new yoga friends, Tsui. Stacey, friend and owner of the yoga studio, called the cops, and they in turn called Boston.

Stacey and Tsui raced from New York to Boston, putting the retreat on hold until the next day. They arrived and found me beaten but alive. After a quick hospital trip, they drove me back to New York to complete my weekend and graduate with the rest of the students.

I was so incredibly grateful to my new friends who had gone out on a limb for me. Meeting genuine people at the retreat almost made the previous two and a half years of hell worth the pain and humiliation I'd endured. But all that was behind me now.

I wanted a change. I wanted to start life on a new page and write my happily ever after. Following the kidnapping and Edwards's subsequent death, the first year had not been easy, and I had not expected it to be. Stacey gave me the use of her tiny condo that she reserved for guest teachers at her studio. I took classes and did what she called karma yoga—when something is given for free, or in exchange for something. In this case, it was the use of her condo.

With no job, I was able to volunteer at her three-room yoga studio. At first, cleaning up and washing floors, helping with bookings and connecting the right teacher and student for private classes. I moved up, eventually becoming an instructor.

A few weeks ago, a fellow teacher and friend, Tino, had invited me to join him on a trip to Turkey. I guess he had assumed by accepting, I also agreed to sex, and when I had made it perfectly clear that I was not interested, he made it perfectly clear that we would go our separate ways.

Fine with me, it was more important to be happy than to lower myself to make others happy. I have done that too many times, and I wasn't about to fall into that trap again. In fact, I had been quite irate at the idea of someone putting stipulations on our mutual travel after the fact. I felt like a newly enlightened yoga chick, and Tino's attitude just didn't fly with me.

Of course, I realized after I'd packed my stuff and found a cheap B&B by the beach that my irritation and condemnation wasn't part of my newly made self, either. That's why I had sought out the beach so late tonight. With everything quiet, I could spend some time in meditation.

I sat down and crossed my legs, resting the backs of my hands comfortably on my thighs. I imagined that my sits bones were like roots that descended deeply into the sand, creating a grounding effect. Then I spread my awareness, becoming more conscious of the earth beneath me and the subtleness of the air that sent tingles up my spine.

The breeze felt like the gentle caress of a lover's hand. I wore a smile on my face, as I often did when I tagged into the subtleties that allowed me to feel the world around me so intensely.

I focused on breathing, my favorite breath of inhaling for five, holding my breath for seven, and exhaling for eight. I called it my anti-anxiety breath, and it only needed to be performed three times to reset one's neurological center. Then I allowed my breath to become deep and natural.

My focus shifted to the subtleties of the breath, becoming aware of cool air moving in and warm air moving out. Each breath was fully circular in nature, with a beginning and an end. As I continued, I lost track of my surroundings, my breath now moving in time with the waves.

With my eyes closed, I gazed internally to the place above the bridge of my nose. It had taken a lot of practice to achieve perfect holding of this meditative gaze point. I had started with candle gazing, called Tratak, and eventually, I was able to imagine a candle flame in the center of my forehead.

Time passed. I couldn't really say how much, as the intention was to get out of linear time and get into the life cycle's eternal time. I felt sufficiently relaxed and centered within myself. My thinking moved to Tino and why I had been so offended by his actions and words. Beyond the obvious, I realized my reaction was because he'd hit a trigger.

I believed that being part of a more sacred community came with a set of responsibilities. I expected more from people. They were, after all, supposed to be highly evolved and beyond typical pitfalls. That was my mistake. I never should have assumed.

Then, he'd tried to control me with sex, something my ex would have done. That wasn't the truth, though; that was my perception. What he'd done was made a huge assumption, and we weren't on the same page. I took a deep breath, and when I let it out, I felt better. Then I thought of the more profound question—was I ready to get back in the saddle? Ready to date, or at least imagine being with a man?

|An image of a gorgeous, primal man flitted into my subconscious. The same face I had dreamt about before leaving New York. In my dream, he held me in his arms, a look of concern marring his brow. He was the most gorgeous mountain of a man I'd ever seen. Then, in the dream, I passed out, and in my bed, I woke up. When I shared it with

my girlfriend Stacey, she had smiled and said I'd been sent a vision of my future.

Tino's invite then seemed like the go light I'd been waiting for. I left New York and felt an eagerness for what was to come, to see new sights and maybe meet someone in Turkey. Well, if he was here, I hoped I'd meet him soon. I sighed and slowly moved away from meditation. I could feel the lateness of the night and knew it was time to get moving.

When I opened my eyes, I glanced down at my phone. It was after midnight and time to get back to my lodgings. I loved my alone time, but I doubted the wisdom of being on the beach at this late hour. I was packing up the few items left strewn on the sand when I heard a grunt.

Peeking over the log behind me, I saw three men on the sand about fifty feet away. Two were standing, one of them pointing a gun at the third guy, who was on his knees in the sand. They had chosen a spot that was dark, the buildings behind them shading their corner of the beach.

Crap! What do I do? If I shout and distract the bad guys, they will no doubt come after me. But I can't let them shoot that poor man, no matter what he's done, assuming he's done anything. Maybe this is just a simple robbery.

I glanced above me, to the full moon overhead. In a moment, the few clouds in the night sky would pass over the moon, shading where I was hiding. I needed a distraction so I could run and hopefully the man being held at gunpoint could as well. I called the police, whispering as loud as I dared, and told them the general location, but I don't know if they even understood me.

With the clouds almost in place, I grabbed a few rocks and stayed low, waiting for the perfect moment. From where I was hiding, I could hear the man on his knees. I assumed from his tone, he was begging for his life. I had no idea what he was saying, but anyone could recognize desperation.

The gunman cocked the gun while the other guy quietly threatened him, in what I recognized now as the Turkish dialect. They wanted information from the guy on his knees, but he wasn't giving up anything.

Just then, the clouds overhead passed over the moon, providing me with an opportunity. I silently thanked Ganesh for providing me with his assistance and, in quick succession, threw the rocks over the men, hitting the stone pavement and a large garbage bin several feet behind them. As they turned, I ran for the boardwalk. I was almost to safety when I heard a shot ring out and men shouting.

I turned back in time to see the man who had been on his knees running down the beach in my direction, with the other two in hot pursuit. Damn man, why couldn't he have run the other way? Behind me, more gunshots rang out, and a bullet ricocheted off a building to my right.

I was desperate as I ran, looking for an open doorway or anyone who could help me, as no sirens were coming to my rescue. At least I could say *yardim*, which meant help. I went tearing around a corner and saw an open bar. Being summer in Turkey, I ran straight in through the open patio, turning for the washroom, when I ran into a wall and would have fallen back onto the tiled floor if the wall hadn't reached out and grabbed my arms.

I gazed up into the face of the most handsome man I'd ever seen. *That figures, I probably just ran into Mr. Perfect, and now I am going to die.*

"Please, help me, there are men with guns. I saw them; they were going to kill someone, and now they are chasing me." I hoped I was imparting the same sense of urgency I was feeling.

The man said something in Turkish to the bartender, who nodded his head and began closing up shop while the wall ducked down the hall, his hands still wrapped around my fore-arms, propelling me out the back door.

We stood in the alley and heard the pounding of feet pass our hiding spot. More gunshots rang out, piercing the quiet. They must still be chasing the man who had escaped, contin-uing the chase no doubt farther into the beachfront commu-nity. I had been panting, more from fear than from the run. I almost died, I almost… I promptly passed out.

Chapter 2

Laughlin

I left the secret society meeting, intent on walking to the beach for some fresh ocean air. We'd been debating for hours on the best course of action in the latest development of the Templars' treasure recovery. I needed quiet to process all the angles presented in the meet.

I was descended from a long line of Templar Knights, now called Freemasons. We met once a year in some undisclosed location, to debate any severe threats or issues and to develop necessary strategies.

Only the master mason, and sometimes his second, attended these annual meetings. I was feeling unsettled and sought the soothing sounds of the sea. I was just stepping out of the men's room when I was slammed in the chest.

I stumbled back, grabbing hold of two arms, attached to the most attractive woman I'd ever seen. She looked at me, terrified, and started mumbling about someone being after her. I had Alfie, our host for the night, quickly close shop and steered the woman out the back door. I was about to call the authorities when I heard running and shouting.

Whoever they were, they passed our spot and continued, a few gun shots ringing out so loud, I would be surprised if the authorities had not already been alerted. I was about to tell the woman in my arms that we were safe when she passed out.

After checking to ensure she was unharmed, I scooped her up and carried her back to my small villa a few blocks away. She must have passed out from the shock. I placed her down on the couch and left her side to grab water and a cool cloth, which I placed on her forehead.

As I gazed down into her lovely face, I tried to remember her eye color. I'd only see them for a moment. What color were they? A shade of green, I thought. She had a light sprinkling of freckles on her fair skin, brown-auburn hair that cascaded halfway down her back, and a toned, hourglass figure… deadly, and precisely to my taste.

I disliked those skinny, blonde Barbie dolls with the fake everything… the whitened teeth were beyond the natural, the false fingernails, eyebrow tints, and lash extensions. Might as well buy a mannequin and install a voice box into it.

The woman lying on my couch was real, her beauty all her own. I found myself fantasizing about what she was like as a person, and more importantly, about how she'd found herself running from gunmen at almost one in the morning.

If she had been mine, there was no way she would be traversing the streets of Turkey alone, dressed in barely-there clothing. She wore a wrap, something one would wear over a bathing suit, and sandals. I felt the skin on her arms. She was freezing. I went to the bedroom and grabbed two throws, covering her up and tucking in her arms and legs.

Better that way, hiding her body kept me from fantasizing about things I shouldn't be thinking about. I was sure this lass was from America, and I was from Scotland, Earl of Roswell, head of Clan Campbell, wealthy landowner, and many other things.

I'd inherited the dynasty at a young age. My father was mysteriously killed while looking into business for the Templars. My mother had passed when I was a young boy, leaving me in my father's hands, who, in turn, leaned heavily on his personal assistant and our maid, Annie.

It wasn't a bad life. It was solitary, as I homeschooled until high school. My father wanted complete control of my education, and the secret heritage and history of Scotland and the Templars played as the primary theme.

I wouldn't say the man had raised me with a healthy dose of trust issues, but everything in our life was such a cloak and dagger that trust had to be gained, not given. Since his passing, I'd been in control of my destiny and liked it that way.

I attended social events that benefited my station and Scotland, giving large amounts of money to charitable organizations, with particular attention paid to the ocean. In school, I'd been fascinated by the sea and had hoped to go into marine biology.

My father dashed those hopes when he told me no respectable lord became a marine biologist. As his only child, I would be inheriting a throne that would allow me to help all of the aquatic biology efforts in the future if I remained steadfast in my seat of power and grew our extensive empire.

And so, I had, with nothing new ever really entering my world. This young woman was the first unexpected mystery to come my way, and I couldn't help but be curious about the nature of her being in Turkey and why she was caught up in gunfire. She was an unknown, and despite my resolve to always stay impartial and away from any woman, other than a one-night stand, I resolved to unravel the one that lay before me and find out more.

I didn't have long to wait. Almost as if hearing my

thoughts, the woman chose that moment to open her eyes. I was right; her shade was green, but her eyes seemed greyer when they moved to take in her surroundings. They roamed back to me, not a trace of fear evident in her expression.

Our eyes held for a moment, and in her depths, I saw a question. Was it a reflection of my own wondering? Then a small smile appeared on her lips. "It's nice to see that the wall I ran into was human. Thank you for helping me. What happened after I, you know, uh, passed out?"

I could tell already that she wasn't a faint-hearted lass. That was good. She was straight forward, moving to the point quickly, instead of batting her eyes and acting as the maiden in distress. I'd had enough of those games in high school and college to last me a lifetime.

"I'm not entirely sure. I was about to call the local authorities when there was more gunfire, and then you fell into my arms, and I brought you to my villa. We are only a few blocks from the bar where you sought refuge."

She sat up, and I handed her the glass of water. She sighed after downing it, a small look of bliss cloyingly displayed on her features. So, she enjoyed simple things. She must be some poor student traveling after college; she certainly didn't look older than twenty-four or so.

"So, lass, what had you involved in a shootout? Why were you running?"

"Perhaps I should save my story for the authorities, then I only have to share it once."

I smirked at her remark. "I am friends with the local gendarme and am happy to escort you there tomorrow. First, I would like to know more about what happened this evening and what sort of trouble you are in."

She sighed and sat back. "Honestly, I don't know if I am in any trouble. I was down on the beach meditating, obviously for a lot longer than I had intended. When I noticed the time, I began to gather my belongings when I heard a sound like a grunt behind me. I peeked over the log where I had been sitting and saw three men. One was on his knees, the other two were standing, and one was holding a gun pointed at the man on his knees. They were talking, but in Turkish, so I didn't know what they were saying, except I was pretty sure that the pair standing wanted to know something from the guy on his knees. I could tell from the way they spoke and gestured with their hands."

She stopped and took a deep breath. "Um, do you happen to have something stronger than water? I could sure use it."

I left her side and filled two crystal goblets with whiskey. I handed her the glass and watched as she raised it to her lips. Her mouth was sensuous, and I was almost envious of the glass. I wondered what her mouth would feel like wrapped around my cock and had to shake my head to get the image out of my mind.

"Anyway, I couldn't let the poor man get shot, but I had nothing with which to defend myself or him."

She was brave, courageous, and completely lacking in self-preservation skills. She was the kind of woman who kept a man on his toes, certainly not the kind I needed in my life.

"I waited until the moon was covered by some clouds and threw some rocks past them so they would turn away from me. When they did, I ran for the boardwalk and into town. What I didn't reckon on was the guy who'd been on his knees fleeing in my direction. Had he gone down the beach, those men wouldn't have even known I was there. I don't know if they could identify me or not."

Oh, how couldn't they? She was perfection, and not many of her could be found in Turkey's little ocean front port. They would be looking for her. She was in danger. "Why are you in Turkey, and are you here with anyone?"

She seemed thoughtful. "I don't think I will answer that if

you don't mind. I have no idea who you are or why you happened to be in that bar alone at almost one in the morning. For all I know, you are a predator."

I laughed. I couldn't help it. If I was a predator at my height of six foot five inches and muscular bulk from hours of training and martial arts, she wouldn't have stood a chance. So American, this one, thinking her lack of confession would keep her safe.

"I am Laughlin Campbell, Lord Erskine and Earl of Roswell, at your service."

She blinked several times and then began laughing. Her laughter was the epitome of merriment, bringing a smile to my lips. Her husky tone contained a hint of tinkling, like a soft bell or the sound of a burbling brook. She seemed to have many sounds wrapped up in her laugh, making her more of a fascination. Everything about his woman was intriguing, even her lack of manners.

"I'm sorry, did I say something amusing?"

"I am many things, Laughlin, but I am not a fool. Are you telling me that I was rescued by one of the most premier peers in all of Scotland?" She'd done her homework and knew the name, so she looked for her bag and, seeing it on the floor by her side, grabbed her phone and quickly did a Google search. Imagine her surprise, when a picture of my mug showed up on her screen.

The 'deer caught in the headlights' look she was brandishing changed my mood instantly from annoyance to amusement. "I apologize, Laughlin, um, Sir, what do I call you?"

She was genuinely curious about whether she was required to acknowledge me by a title, but when her gorgeous mouth uttered the word Sir, I felt my cock stir. "Laughlin will suffice, lass. Now answer my questions, and if you lie, you will have lost the privilege of calling me by my first name, then only Sir will suffice."

Years of sitting at my father's right hand had taught me how to control others and create a favorable outcome. She seemed shocked, not knowing if I was joking or serious. I had been joking, but before I could allow her to see my amusement, she seemed to become acutely aware of my proximity to her.

My hip rested gently against her thigh. She moved to the floor and sat cross-legged. I missed her heat and tried not to look longingly at her from the safe distance she'd created between us. She took a deep breath, as if to ready herself for something. With her eyes closed once more, I could take in her beauty.

She was different. I could tell from the way she interacted with her environment. She was very connected to her world and not bound by things that clouded other women. She was very singular and independent but not in a way that screamed women's rights, more in a way that spoke divine feminine. She didn't need a sign or to walk in a protest to show who she was or what she believed in.

When her eyes opened, I noticed they were greener than they had been lying on the couch, as if by sitting on the floor, she increased an internal vibrancy that affected her eye color. She regarded me with a mix of curiosity and trepidation. She had been hurt. I could see that in the way she held herself away from me.

It wasn't fear that did that, at least not fear of me. It was a more general distrust of men. I kept my face impassive; I was good at not giving away my thoughts when concealing them was required.

"My name is Suri." A lie, but I would not dig yet. I wanted more first.

"Nice to meet you, Suri."

She answered with a small smile and continued. "I'm a widow, about a year now, and I'm here on vacation. I was with a friend, but we parted ways, and I moved into a small B&B on the beachfront for the remainder of my trip. I was annoyed with my friend for trying to initiate something with me, and I fear I was rather harsh in my judgment. I was at the beach to, uh, well, to meditate. I'm sure that sounds stupid to you, but it's what I do when I need to process things, or I get bogged down."

So, I was dealing with an injured bird with self-regulation issues. That was so much better than image issues and drug or alcohol problems. Meditation sounded like a profoundly gratifying practice for Suri. Just seeing her perched on the floor, she seemed more in control of herself than lying down on my couch.

Her cheeks pinkened at her words. I almost felt like a thief who had stolen from her more than she'd planned on sharing. "I see, so you are here vacationing. Welcome to Turkey." She grinned and did a little bow of her head. "Thank you, Lord Roswell, and why are you here?"

What was safe to share? That I found her intoxicating? That I was the head of a sect formerly known as the Templar Knights? That I was here as part of my title, but my personal reasons were to find information about my father's untimely death? What could I share?

The cover I needed bloomed in my mind like a flower, and I grabbed hold of it. "Business, marine business, actually. I spend the day negotiating back and forth with environmental groups and marine biology heads, here at Mayis University. You could say the environment is an issue close to my heart. Our seas are polluted, and the great mechanisms of today's technology avoid the necessary changes to fix the issue before our seas are completely lost."

I knew this would interest her, and I could talk for days

about the environment and the issue we were facing as a planet. Suri audibly gulped, and when she spoke, her voice had become huskier. Damn, the woman was turned on by what I said. Oh, she was a delight, and how I wished I could play with her for the rest of her vacation and then simply wave goodbye.

But I knew better. She was different, and as much as I wanted her, I knew I couldn't have her. I was dominant and enjoyed darker pursuits in my downtime. If she gave herself to me, I might just have to break my oath to myself of not getting involved with women and take this one home with me.

"I see. That is commendable. I am not familiar with European philanthropy, but I am glad you are pursuing worthy causes. I, well, my husband's family was rich, and their philanthropic projects centered around whatever was in fashion. I found it all quite hard to swallow."

Unwittingly, Suri had supplied me with enough information to find out her identity and her background. There was still a chance she was not telling the truth. If anyone after the Templars' secrets wanted to get to me, why not use a beautiful woman? It worked in all those James Bond movies.

I decided I needed to keep Suri close until I knew more. If she was a spy, I would find out who she worked for. If she was who she said she was, I would need to keep her safe, at least until we knew who the three men from the beach were.

"Suri, I would like you to stay here for tonight. If those men can identify you, they can find out where you are staying. From the sounds of it, they are local and can garner information if they need to. Once we know more, it may be safe for you to return."

She was about to argue with me, and I held up my hand. She stopped immediately. That made my cock jump in my pants again. This woman, despite her independence, had a streak of submissiveness that drew me.

"I have a guest room and all the toiletries you require. Come, I will show you to your room. You can shower and clean up, while I will grab a t-shirt for you to sleep in."

She put up no argument as I led her to the guest room and left to find her a shirt.

When I was done, I said my goodnights and closed her door, wishing I could lock it from this side. I was not interested in hosting a prisoner, but her free-spirited nature could get her into trouble. I, too, had a shower and climbed into the cool sheets, closing my eyes. My sleep was troubled. Images of gunmen kept me tossing and turning until a knock on my bedroom door drew me from the restless sleep back to the present. What could she possibly want?

Chapter 3

Suri

Holy *crap!* He was the guy from my dream I'd had before leaving New York. He was even better looking in person. No wonder he'd felt like a wall when I'd run into him earlier, as he had massive proportions.

When he smiled, I saw him as the big bad wolf. His wolfish grin and the intensity of his glittering eyes, I'd rarely seen from a man. His closeness had rendered me unable to answer his questions. I had to move to the floor and move my body away from his energy.

The man positively vibrated with masculine energy, and then there was his scent. He was a blend of so many things, it overwhelmed me. He was not just tall, but his width made two of me, and I was not a small, nor petite woman.

I had muscles from my college running days and, after a year of yoga, had toned my Marilyn Monroe figure by engaging in daily sessions. I could tell that Laughlin liked what he saw, and that made me even more nervous. I felt like his prey, but even that vibe wasn't wholly descriptive.

I'd felt like a target with Edward, but in his case, I was more of a victim and the last one to see it. This guy had honed his primal side and wasn't afraid to show what he liked, oozing confidence that fit with his striking appearance.

He was more man than I'd ever had the pleasure of getting to know. He was the type of man who could make love for hours. If his massive biceps and thighs said anything, he was in shape and trained regularly. But I think he did more than train with weights. He was dangerous, like he had fought in matches, or perhaps real life.

When I'd run into him, he had barely stumbled back, almost as if he was prepared. But how could he be? How could he know some crazy woman was about to turn the corner at full speed? Had his instincts been so honed that he knew to prep himself for the impact? I found him fascinating and wanted to learn how his pieces were put together.

Lying in his guest bed, wearing a shirt that smelled like him, was too intoxicating to allow sleep. All I wanted was to lie in his arms, which had felt like a warm, safe haven earlier when he caught me. Being in his shirt, his smell was doing all kinds of crazy things to my libido. An hour later, I couldn't take it any longer.

I got out of bed and tiptoed down to his room, gently knocking on the door. I was fully prepared to run back to my room, a chicken, if he didn't answer me right away.

"Suri, are you all right, lass?"

I felt my lady parts squeeze in response to his voice. That soft Scottish bur was enough to make me crawl on my knees to his side. " Um, may I come in?"

"Of course, lass." He turned on the light and blinked owlishly from the bed.

"I hate to bother you, but, well, I can't sleep. I'm a little afraid. Do you mind if I, uh, join you? Just to sleep, of course."

His face remained passive as he lifted the cover and invited me in, but when he pulled me into a spoon position, I could feel just how much of an effect my ass had on him. I was going to protest, but he turned off the light, tucked me tightly to him, wrapping his massive arm around me. I felt so safe that I drifted off immediately.

I was not one to sleep for long periods, but I did sleep deeply. When I awoke, the sun was just rising. I could see the pale light through the cracks in the blinds. I slid out from the warmth of the bed, immediately regretting my decision.

Shivering in the coolness of the dawn, I tiptoed back to my room. Laughlin had left me women's yoga pants on the bed, and when I pulled them on under his long t-shirt, they fit perfectly.

Figures, he is probably a rake, like my dead husband was. Probably has women stationed all over Europe, just like Edward had women all over the United States.

I was going to leave. I had told Laughlin the location of the B&B. If he really needed to find me, he could. But then I thought of those men and the gun and decided I'd wait on that until he was fully awake and had shared his plan with me.

Instead, I made coffee and took a cup with me out to the deck. The sun was cresting the water, and it was stunning, a sight I don't think I could ever tire of. After my coffee, I grabbed one of the throws from last night and placed it out on the sand beyond his deck.

I sat down and did some breathing, and soon I was ready to begin my morning salutations. I did six rounds of Surya Namaskar, commonly known as sun salutations. Each full rotation brought a new level of nimbleness to my limbs. I went through the warrior poses next and then lay down on the blanket to stretch. I had to keep my glutes stretched out, or they tightened up too much and caused me hip pain.

There was still no Laughlin in sight when I was done, so I

stripped off my clothes and headed into the water. I hadn't seen anyone as yet and assumed his villa came with a private beach. I was fine, either way, and I hadn't read anything, any rules, against topless bathing.

I dove into the waves and delighted in the feel of the watery world in which I swam. A school of dolphins quite a way out from where I was swimming was passing by. They were so beautiful, I wished I could swim with them, but my swim skills were limited to shallow waters only.

So, instead, I sent a silent salute to the animals then chanted a little. I could have been mistaken, but they seemed to take notice of me and slowed down their progress. *Oh yes*, I silently prayed that they would come closer.

They did, and then about thirty feet out, they stopped, their heads bobbing, their permanent smiles making them look like a group of happy travelers. "Hello, beautiful ones," I crooned, hoping they understood how in awe I was of their beauty. They stared a moment longer and then, chittering, continued on their way.

I watched them until they were mere pinpoints on the horizon. Then I turned to swim back to shore. And there he was, casually leaning against the deck railing, coffee in hand in nothing but a pair of shorts.

Holy crap, the man was a god, housed in the perfect meat suit. If I came away from this without having sex, I would consider myself to have enviable self-control skills. But did I want to? I stared at him and held his eye as I stalked up the sand, naked except for my underwear. Grabbing the blanket from the sand, I wrapped it around myself. And without so much as a word, I walked by Laughlin and headed to the shower.

Once I was safely ensconced in hot water, I let out the breath I'd been holding since I exited the ocean. Leaning against the shower wall, I attempted to get my bearings. Wow, he was something else. The way he'd been watching me sent a shiver down my spine. That Earl of Roswell had an intensity that turned me into a pool of liquid.

I wanted him, I honestly did, but the idea of having sex with such a powerful man was intimidating. I exited the guest room in my clothing from yesterday, to find Laughlin in the kitchen making breakfast. He glanced up when he heard me. "Morning, lass, fruit salad good for you?"

"Yes, thank you, that sounds perfect."

He placed down two bowls of exotic fruit, freshly whipped cream, and a carafe of coffee. I picked up my fork and was about to take a bite when Laughlin spoke. "Did I not make it clear that you were in danger and to stay here?"

I glanced up from my bowl, only to see that wolfish look of his. The intensity shook me to my core. At this rate, I'd be crawling on the floor begging for his forgiveness. I needed to get myself under control.

"I'm sorry, was that a statement or a question?" I held his gaze, not backing down. His eyes glittered dangerously. Holy crap, if I wasn't careful, this could escalate into something I wasn't sure I'd recover from.

"Is that meant as a question, lass, or as a rebellion against your host?"

Damn, now I feel guilty. This man could make me feel like an errant child. I'd never been around anyone so self-possessed and in control of themselves.

"My apologies, Lord Roswell," I said with a bow of my head and a smirk.

His eyes narrowed. "You seem to have a knack for polite avoidance. I warn ye, lass. I am a very dominant man who always gets his way. I will not stand for your blatant and deliberate disregard of my orders, which were made for your safety and certainly not for my comfort."

I'd had enough. I stood up and headed for the front door.

Before I could reach the handle, Laughlin grabbed me and threw me over his shoulder as he stalked back into the main living space.

"Let go of me, you brute. I'm not even here because I want to be. I can take care of myself; now let me down." Laughlin sat down on the couch and pulled me over his knee. Oh no, he didn't. "Really? How archaic are you? Get out of the dark ages, you—"

Before I could utter another word, Laughlin's hand came down on my backside. His massive hand quickly administered a few dozen hard spanks. I was grunting and swearing, becoming something I'd never been before, petulant and dually remorseful at the same time. His spanking was creating the worst heat imaginable.

"Stop it!" I cried out repeatedly, on deaf ears. I'd never been spanked before, and the experience was shocking. It hurt more than I ever imagined it could, and it was making me feel things I generally shut off or did yoga to let go of.

"Please, please, oh god, it hurts, please, Laughlin. I promise I won't be disrespectful, just please stop." My ass was on fire, and I was so embarrassed that I wanted to crawl under the nearest piece of furniture.

He didn't stop, and I found myself wondering how many women he'd spanked. He knew what he was doing and paid a lot of attention to where my thighs and buttocks met. No doubt I wouldn't be sitting comfortably for a few days.

Eventually, the fight went out of me, and I hung limply over his large thighs until he finished. I was surprised to find that, emotionally, I felt like I'd had a reset button pressed. The events of last night, even the irritation about Tino, had evaporated.

Of course, I had these thoughts as a few tears slid down my cheeks. In a way, I felt safer than I'd ever felt before. But there was no way I would let him know that. Laughlin righted me and looked me in the eyes. " Are you ready to be you and not some spoilt, bratty girl?"

I wanted to argue, to ask him who the hell he thought he was calling me spoilt and bratty. One thing was for sure, I wasn't spoiled. I wasn't sure about bratty. If he meant stubborn, then he was correct.

"Yes."

"Yes, what?"

"Uh, I'm not sure, yes, Sir?"

Laughlin's face broke into an amused smile. He shook his head as he gazed at me. "You are something, lass. I love your spirit."

I wiped a stray tear from my cheek. "Thank you, I guess. Is that a compliment?"

He laughed, a loud guffawing sound erupting from him so quickly, it startled me, and I jumped, falling from his lap to the floor. As I landed with a *thud*, Laughlin laughed harder, and I joined, the entire scene so comical.

When we both had calmed down, Laughlin stood and pulled me to my feet. Grabbing a throw cushion from the couch, he drew me back to the kitchen and breakfast. Laughlin placed the soft padding on my chair and gestured for me to sit down.

I did, gingerly, and he pushed in my chair. Then taking the one opposite me, he poured us coffee and began chatting like nothing had happened. Who was this guy? All through breakfast, my core, which had become molten lava with the spanking, much to my embarrassment, needed release.

Why couldn't he have just taken and ravished me instead of creating this need in me? "Do you have meetings today, Lord Roswell?"

He grinned at me. "Laughlin, lass, unless you're naughty, then Lord Roswell, or Sir, will do."

Seriously? My lady parts squeezed in response to his

words. What was wrong with me? I knew the guy was gorgeous and clearly well educated, with the body of a god—to summarize, a total hottie.

"And in response to your question, I have called my contact at the station. No gunshots were reported last night."

I was shocked. How? "I called them from the beach, and we clearly heard them. It was so loud, how could no one else have heard?"

Laughlin studied me as if he was choosing what to say in response to my sudden outburst. I started to see that I was more dramatic than I realized, or maybe he brought it out in me. I found that being around Laughlin, I wasn't as evolved as I'd been giving myself credit for these past few months. The realization was like being doused by a bucket of water.

He observed me with a quiet concentration I found discomforting. "Lass, do you have anything else to tell me? Are you sure there is no more to your story?"

I thought back over the events of last night. "No, I'm sorry, that is all I know. As I said, I didn't understand what was being said, but I did recognize the language spoken was Turkish."

Laughlin seemed to have made up his mind. "There are only a few reasons why a call wouldn't be made. If the residents knew something was going down in advance, which screams local mafia. Or the citizens had been silenced after the fact, which would also be mafia but not necessarily local."

I felt faint, and I must have looked it because Laughlin's look changed from one of frankness to empathy.

"But, Laughlin, I called them from the beach, now that I think about it. Shouldn't I have heard sirens as I ran from the beach for safety?"

"Don't worry, lass. I have connections here, and we will get to the bottom of things. Come, why don't you have a rest, and we'll pick this up after you've had a chance to relax."

Laughlin scooped me up in his arms. I snuggled into his

warmth, not realizing how cold I'd been. It must be the shock, a part of my brain registered. When Laughlin laid me down, I gazed up into his fathomless eyes, begging for him to stay to make me warm.

Without a word, he lay down and pulled me in tight, like last night, and held me. Breathing in his scent was like a balm, and I fell asleep almost instantly.

Chapter 4

Laughlin

With the lass safe and sleeping soundly, I tiptoed out of the bedroom and into my temporary office. I spent the next hour typing encrypted emails and sending them out to my fellow master masons here in Turkey.

In addition to that, feeling that the lass needed some semblance of her life restored while we ascertained the level of danger she may be in, I booked dinner with my best friend and fellow Templar, Marc, and his current flavor, Sophie.

Marc was an engaging rogue, who had the gift of gab and a bevy of beauties to prove it. Unlike me, who usually paid for services to keep things in my life uncluttered with drama, Marc had a new girlfriend every two to three months.

We'd been brought up in the order together, becoming friends in our later teen years. Marc was short for Marcus Williams, Duke of Monteros and Earl of Pemsheild. King Stephen of England was his ancestor on his father's side and he had Scottish royalty on his mother's side.

Unlike me, Marc had no problem using his lineage to get in the pants of some of the most beautiful women in the world. Attractive, if you liked plastic Barbie dolls. I booked dinner and then found Suri's B&B. I had Alfie send his son to the location, only a few blocks away, to gather her belongings and bring them here.

Then I called in a favor and, based on pure speculation, ordered some clothing to be delivered from Antalya to the hidden gem, Selimiye, where we were currently residing. She would need proper attire for dinner. Then I snuck back into the bedroom and found her once again missing.

What was it with this woman? Had she no preservation skills whatsoever? Back out and through the kitchen door, I found her on the patio, this time in my t-shirt. She sat gazing out at sea, her mind clearly a million miles away.

The deck was partially blocked, but the sun had found its way to her, lighting up her skin. She looked ethereal, shimmered in the sun. I wanted to reach out and touch her to make sure she was real, but I pulled back and contented myself with observing.

She had appeared brilliant and remote by moonlight last night. But in the sun, her edges softened and blended, giving her the appearance of a watercolor painting. I desired to drown myself in her essence, taste her, smell her, take her. Suri must have felt me staring, for she rewarded me with a lazy smile.

"I see I will have to put a tracker on ye for your own safety." I said it lightly so as not to upset her. She seemed much more in control than earlier, and I wanted to get to know her and enjoy an evening of wine and food and, of course, get Marc's opinion of her story.

She moved into a folded position, her ass aimed at me, then slowly dove up towards the sun before straightening. "It is so beautiful here. I do love the beach, and rarely have I made the trip to be on or by it since high school."

She stalked towards me, and as she passed, her hand brushed my cock. She tensed at the contact, but I knew she'd done it on purpose. I grabbed her, swinging her body towards me—a soft *whoomph* released from her as our bodies gently collided.

She gazed up into my eyes, her pupils dilated and her breath short and breathy. I was in a place I'd never allowed myself since my college days, a decade ago. Women were complicated. It was why I paid top dollar for my enjoyment. I never wanted again to be accused of something I didn't do. I couldn't afford public defamation of character.

I hadn't kissed a woman in years, but her plump cherry lips called to me like a siren's call. Leaning down, I took her chin in a gentle grip. Stooping to accommodate our almost foot difference in height, I gently kissed her. Her taste sent a force through my body that I had never experienced. She returned my attentions with a vigor, gripping me and pulling me in tight.

My eyes popped open. I had rarely ever been touched and not with so much ferocity and energy. I growled deep in my throat, wanting to take Suri hard and swift. She moaned in my mouth as my tongue plundered her, sipping from her sweetness.

I ran my hands down her sides and gripped her bottom, her cheeks still warm from her spanking. She moaned deeply, her head dropping back. I took the opportunity to plant kisses and gentle bites down her neck.

Needing a better space, I scooped her up and made for my room. I deposited her on the bed and climbed on, with our lips never parting. Suri used a combination of flexibility and strength to wrap her legs around my hips and roll on top.

Oh god, she was glorious with her head thrown back in

ecstasy. I reached up and took her breasts in my hands, groaning as I thumbed her nipples. She mewled like a kitten when I gently pinched them. Her skin was soft and malleable. I could lose myself just by touching her.

I moved her hips until she was stationed above my shaft, and then I plunged in, like a desperate pirate looking for treasure, and I found it between her legs. She rode me hard, a change to what I was used to doing.

Encouraging her, I swirled one of my digits around her clit. Her breathing hitched to a higher gear, becoming harsh and fast as she chased her first orgasm. Feeling her walls clench, I tweaked her nipple and pressed down on her clit. Her essence gushed all over my cock, her strong walls milking me hard. I didn't know how long I could last. The little minx was clearly in deep need of release and didn't even slow down as she rode the wave to her next orgasm.

Using my size and strength, I flipped us over and hammered into her, pressing her knees into her shoulders with my chest. With no space to move, she was open to me, and I took her.

"Oh, god, Laughlin, yes, please... just like that," she got out in a fragmented sentence, the intensity of her feelings taking over.

Suri's orgasm overwhelmed her as she thrashed her head from side to side, screaming my name as she did. My dark side took over. This woman wanted me, and I wouldn't deny her. I flipped her onto her knees, and she dropped down onto her forearms, arching her gorgeous, voluptuous ass at me.

I gave her ass two smacks quickly and then grasped her hips, plowing into her beautiful weeping gap. I pushed her chest down, increasing the angle and hitting her G-spot with each stroke. Suri was crying out her orgasm in seconds, her strong muscles milking me, and I was fast on my way to following her release.

As her orgasm crested and she trembled with the aftermath, I roared out my own release, eliciting one more from her. Her hot sheath pulled and massaged my member, drawing out my ejaculation.

When I was finally done, I dropped down on the bed and pulled her in tightly this time. Unlike our previous two snuggle sessions, this wasn't about comfort. Our fronts towards each other, Suri rested her face on my bicep. It took another minute for our breathing to regulate.

It was at that moment, the doorbell rang. *That must be Alfie's kid with Suri's stuff.* "Wait here," I said, scrambling off the bed and grabbing my robe. I also took my gun from the bathroom drawer and cautiously made my way to the door.

Looking at the security feed, it was indeed Alfie's boy, surrounded by a backpack and a few parcels. My other delivery had also arrived—perfect timing. I opened the door and took everything, promising recompense later. Then picking up the bags, I carried them to the bedroom.

"What's all this? Is that my bag?"

"Yes, I had your things packed up. Don't worry; your bill is paid, and you are freed from your week's contract."

She seemed stunned and stared at me owlishly, her eyes wide and blinking.

"Don't fret, lass, we're going on a date. In fact, we have just enough time to clean up if we want to be on time."

Her curiosity quickly changed to fear. "Do you think it's safe?"

"It is where we're going. Come, let's get cleaned up."

Chapter 5

Suri

Holy hell! *I've just had the best sex of my life.* I wasn't sure how I felt about having my items packed up and brought over without my express permission. But I also realized that Laughlin was the type of man who operated as a problem solver.

He confirmed in the shower that he didn't feel right about leaving me alone and exposed until I'd had time to go over some photos and see if I could identify the gunmen. I conceded that for now, it made the most sense. If things got out of hand, I could always leave.

Laughlin left me to finish after lathering up my body and wringing a few more orgasms out of me with his exquisite fingers. I thought about the sex we'd just had and couldn't believe how much chemistry we had. It was like the massive Scottish lord was made just for me.

He was large in every way, but we fit so perfectly that each stroke of his cock was like an internal massage. I couldn't imagine not having strings of orgasms with the way he worked his member.

When I exited the bathroom, I saw a red cocktail dress on the bed, with matching ballet flats. The material was so soft, I knew it would feel amazing. I put it on and then went back to the bathroom to check out my reflection.

The dress fit perfectly. I added some mala beads that matched my eyes and then did an upsweep with my hair and wove in some tiny seashells for effect. Being a minimalist, I added only mascara and lip gloss to complete my look. I slid my feet into the ballet flats and exited the bedroom.

Laughlin was standing with a glass of wine in his hand, looking out at the ocean. The sky was in its beginning stages of changing to dusk, and the light filters played on his features, adding to the severity of his resting face.

He turned when he heard me, his eyes lighting up like a torch in a cave. "Suri, you look stunning. Thank you for wearing the dress. How does it feel?"

"Like a soft glove, to be honest; you couldn't have chosen a better fit. Thank you."

"Here, lass, I poured you a glass of Chablis. To unexpected adventures," he said, clinking my glass with his. I took a sip of the delicious wine and could only imagine it was as expensive as was everything else he surrounded himself with.

His wealth, while impressive, did nothing for me. I had come from modest wealth and married into one of the wealthiest families in Boston. I had purposely pulled away from the lifestyle that came with wealth because I had found it so empty.

But listening to Laughlin, one could do many good things with wealth when one had the right attitude and a heart for sharing, and he certainly had that. He hadn't done all of this to impress me. He'd done it for my comfort, and that was admirable. He'd removed stressors from me by seeing to my needs, and for that, I was grateful.

"To kind men who rescue maidens," I said, holding up my glass. His eyes darkened, but he returned the cheer. Minutes later, we left for the beach club to meet with his friend Marc and his girlfriend Sophie.

Laughlin and I arrived at the restaurant to find Marc and Sophie already seated. Marc had the wine ordered and breathing and seemed in the process of sharing something amusing with his date. As we approached, she erupted with laughter. I enjoyed the merriment pouring from their table and my reservations about our evening vanished.

We hugged, as we greeted each other like old friends, and sat down. Marc poured the wine and immediately started regaling us with amusing stories from his life. Sophie hung on every word he uttered. As I sat, observing everyone, I learned something new. I realized that this past year had not been about growth, as I had previously thought.

My past year had been about cocooning and healing. Right now, and this entire trip, in fact, was forcing me to grow. If I'd know that Tino and I would part ways and I would end up witnessing an almost murder and end up in the arms of a rich Scottish lord, would I have come?

I wanted to think I would have. Thankfully, I had not known, and here I was, with people who had clearly been living in this world, if not all, at least most of their lives.

"Suri, Earth to Suri, hello."

I was startled out of my deep thoughts to find all three of them staring at me.

"Are you ready to order, love?"

It was only then I noticed the waitress also staring.

"How about I order for everyone? I have a thought on some delights that my taste buds have been fantasizing about all day." Marc winked, causing a deep blush to spread up my neck and face.

Laughlin laid his big paw over mine, like he was claiming me. Marc noticed, and a glint of mischievousness gleamed in his eyes. I glanced up to Laughlin, who was glaring at Marc. It was hard not to laugh at the two friends, boys—men—was there a difference?

By the time we ordered our third bottle of wine, we all seemed to be in the same place, and communication was no longer strained and led solely by Marc. "Suri, other than hanging around with this giant lug, what do you do, from where do you hail, love?"

"My family is from Boston; my parents still live there. I moved to New York a year ago. I needed a change, and a friend offered me a place to stay while I was making the transition."

"Boston is a beautiful city. I like New York as well. The party never ends there. Very different from Scotland." We all laughed at Marc's comment.

"So why New York? Did you leave behind an old life in Boston?"

I felt Laughlin beside me straighten a little, almost as if he didn't like Marc asking me questions, but he didn't say anything, so I continued.

"My husband died suddenly. At that point, I'd been in an unhappy marriage for two years, with barely a shred of self-confidence left. At the same time, I left what I had thought was my dream job in Boston as a corporate fundraiser. My ex was my boss, and I made him look good, and I was fine with it initially. But if I received accolades, he would fly into a rage and usually hurt me. I took my small savings and moved into my friend Shelley's tiny condo. I've been taking courses, learning and teaching yoga, and basically healing since I arrived there."

I stopped and took a big swig of wine. "Honestly, if you had asked me yesterday, I would have said that I've been in the process of transforming and truly living for the first time. But I realized tonight that I've been cocooning."

I meant to only answer Marc's question, yet here I was confessing like a criminal. My eyes became glassy with unshed tears. "I have never traveled; this is my first time on a vacation, and even that had a rocky start."

Laughlin squeezed my hand encouragingly.

"Then I *literally* ran into Laughlin." Marc and Sophie laughed. "Now, here I am with you all, very surreal. Life is a strange journey, don't you think?"

"That's what I love about you yanks, always so expressive." That broke the tension as we all laughed.

"So back in New York, you teach yoga?" Sophie inquired.

"Well, yes, and I recently started a private Reiki practice."

"Oh," Sophie said as she sat up excitedly. "Can you show us how it works? I've only read about it, and I'm so curious."

"It's not ideal to do it when you're drinking; sometimes it impedes the energy, but I will try. Give me your hand."

Sophie gave me her hand, and I placed her palm on my right hand and hovered my left about an inch above hers. I closed my eyes and channeled the healing energy. I didn't expect much, but I felt a rush sizzle up my spine and down my arms. The kundalini had moved very quickly, which meant that the vessel, Sophie, needed healing. That was odd, as she was so young and looked so healthy.

As I allowed the pulsating energy to move through me and into her, I scanned, looking for the source of need. And my eyes opened suddenly, looking into hers. "You have had some issues with your hormones and were considering a hysterectomy. Don't, as this is simply blocked energy, and I can help you. Surgery should always be the last option."

Everyone had gone deathly quiet. Sophie stared at me in wonder. "How the... what are you?"

I was suddenly very embarrassed, as I was a new practitioner and had never seen someone's problem as clearly as I'd seen hers, I thought maybe I was wrong.

"I'm sorry," I apologized. "I shouldn't have said anything, and I'm probably wrong." I dropped my gaze, suddenly wishing the floor would open and swallow me up. This was a problem for me, and now I remembered why the yoga community was so safe. It was different there and was accepted.

"Can you really help me? You are right, and I really don't want the surgery, but my doctor made me feel like there were no other options."

I looked up to Laughlin for guidance. His gaze was filled with a boldness I didn't usually possess outside of the studio where I worked. It emboldened me. "Can she come to your place tomorrow, Laughlin?"

"We have a flight booked for noon and will be gone for two nights. How about when we get back?" Laughlin spoke directly to Marc and Sophie. I wanted to ask where we were going, but he squeezed my hand as a warning that he would tell me later. Maybe he wanted it to be a secret.

"Well, love birds," Marc said, standing and throwing money down on the table, "it's been fun, but my bed is calling me."

We stood and made tentative plans for that weekend, and then we parted ways. Laughlin held my hand as we walked the mile of beachfront back to his villa.

"That's quite a gift you have, lass. I guess it goes with your new name." I should have known he would learn about me. Laughlin wasn't the type of man to keep wayward women around if he didn't know them.

"Suri was granted to me by my yogi friend Shelley. I liked it so much that I decided to make it permanent."

Laughlin smiled down at me. "I understand what it is to need change. It is fine. So, who were you? What was your name before becoming the moon goddess?"

"I was born Mary Stamos, and when I married Edward, I became Mary Stanhope. I have now converted to my new name and taken my mother's maiden name, Suri Sinclair. You see, I have some Scottish in me too."

Chapter 6

Laughlin

Coincidence? The Sinclairs had been part of the Knights Templar story since day one, along with my family, our connection running back to the beginning. I would send the names Suri had provided me with to our head investigator and make a meeting upon our return while Suri was busy with Sophie, assuming Sophie was still in Turkey in a few days. I didn't want to tell Suri Marc's background and, instead, allowed her to formulate her own opinion.

As if reading my thoughts, she said, "Your friend Marc is quite a tease, isn't he? Doesn't seem like the sort to have a woman stay around for long."

I let out a rare full laugh, startling Suri. "You have surmised him well, and yes, I'm afraid our Marc is a total rake. He changes girlfriends every six to eight weeks and has, since being a young lad."

We walked for a few minutes in silence, then she asked,

"Sophie, she seems quite young? I mean, even for her age, she doesn't appear very worldly."

I nodded in agreement. "Sophie does come across as lacking depth, but she is a nice woman despite that. I don't expect she will be around much longer, as five weeks have already passed. Tonight, I could tell that Marc's interest is already waning. You see, despite Sophie being his type, blonde Barbie doll with not a lot going on upstairs, Marc prefers his women ignorant and then swoops in, wines and dines and treats them to what he says is the best sex of their life and then dumps them."

Suri seemed lost in thought as we crested the deck to the villa. The moon chose that moment to peek out from behind its cloud cover, and Suri was caught in its full reflection. Like in the sunlight, she appeared ethereal, the light reflecting on her skin making her appear as a pale goddess.

I gazed from her to the ocean. "Care for a late-night swim, moon goddess?" She looked at me, perplexed. "That's the second time you called me that. Dare I ask?"

I didn't respond.

"Yes, to the swim, please. What a perfect night to be in the embrace of the sea." She took a long breath and let it out slowly, her face tilted to the moon. Did she even know how gorgeous she was?

I found myself intrigued by how Suri viewed the world, people, and, well, anything really. The more I learned, the more I wanted to know. I had never wanted to know anything about anyone, at least, not since school.

I grabbed some towels from the bathroom and placed them on the deck. Turning off all the house lights, we stripped down and, hand in hand, raced towards the water. Diving under the gentle waves, we came up laughing and sputtering.

"Oh my gosh, it is beautiful out here tonight. Thank you,

Laughlin, for such a wonderful evening. Now, tell me where we're going tomorrow."

"Istanbul, you're a tourist after all, and I thought I could take you to the Blue Mosque."

She squealed with delight. "But isn't that a nine-hour drive? Is it worth it?"

I tried not to laugh at her ignorance. But really, did she think I looked like a man who would drive for nine hours when I had a private jet at my disposal? "Suri, you are a true delight, you know that? Remember, we aren't driving; we are flying. We'll be there in half an hour."

She looked shocked. "Half an hour?" she squeaked.

"And don't pack; we are shopping locally. It should be fun. I haven't been in years, but I remember that it was massive, one of the largest markets of its kind in the world. We won't get it all done in one night."

Suri looked troubled. Whatever was on her mind, she was keeping it to herself for the moment. Being a foot taller than Suri, I could stand on the bottom while she had been treading water since we breached the surface. I reached out and pulled her to me. She took the bait and wrapped her arms around my neck and her toned legs around my waist.

I slid one finger inside her warm opening as I leaned down and took her mouth with mine. She moaned and gently rubbed her hips as I pillaged her soft folds. With the buoyant water doing most of the work of holding her up, I was able to lay her back on the waves, her legs still entwined around my waist.

I pulled her down on top of my cock and played with her pebbled nipples. She let her arms float and arched her back as if she was trying to lift her breasts to my palms. I pinched them, eliciting a mewl of need from my little goddess.

Gently grinding my hips against hers, my cock pumped her while I alternated between stroking her breasts and pinching her nipples. Her breath had been coming out in soft pants, but every time I pinched, she squealed and squeezed my cock. Not ready to let her release, I worked on stoking a fire deep within her, and this time, I would control all of her reactions.

"Oh my, Laughlin, that feels so good."

"Does it? Well, there is plenty more, but you must be good."

Her eyes flew open, but she didn't look angry, only more curious. "What do you mean, good?"

"You will not release until I say so. If you listen to me and do what you're told, I will give you multiple orgasms."

She looked genuinely confused. "I don't understand why you wouldn't do that anyway?"

I changed her position, turning her so her back was against my chest, and stretched her arms to encircle my neck. Now I was in a better place to control how I built her passion. "I know you don't understand, but you will. You see, I want to deliver your sensations and keep you dancing at the knife's edge before I cut you loose and allow you to fly. Give yourself to me, Suri, and I will deliver the pleasure that you have never experienced."

As I waited for her to answer, I lifted her and put her back on my cock. I rubbed her hardened nub, and she cried out with pleasure. Then I stopped. "Well, what will it be, my moon goddess?"

"What do I do?" she asked with a sultry, breathy quality.

"Submit to me and do as I say. That is all you need to do."

"Okay, Laughlin, I trust you." And there it was, she gave me a gift with those words, something others had given to me only in play, in exchange for rewards. Suri only wanted what I could deliver, nothing more, and nothing less. She asked for nothing but took what was given. I could fall in love with this woman.

Chapter 7

Suri

L aughlin buckled me into my seat. Ever the gentleman, he looked after me before tending to himself. Once I was comfortable, he opened a bottle of wine that had been chilling, "Cheers to a few fun days."

"Cheers," I responded as the jet took off. It felt like only moments later, as we polished off our second glass, the plane started its descent. "That was super-fast. To think all these years, all I was missing was a private jet."

Laughlin laughed and said, "Mi casa, su casa."

But was it? His comment inspired the opposite effect than was implied. Things were steamy between us, very steamy. I wanted an *us*, and I didn't want *us*, and I didn't know what he wanted. Not knowing his thoughts on *us*, was beginning to wear on me.

We checked into the White House Hotel, a splendid five star, with a stunning view of the city and only a few minutes' walk from the mosque market. Once we checked in, we went for lunch at the Old House Restaurant. Searching on my phone, I found it had a top cuisine rating, with a fun atmosphere.

From the Old House deck, we had a great view of the harbor and city. The atmosphere was casual and relaxing, and I felt it was a great place to bring up my earlier reservations regarding his comment last evening on our walk back to his bungalow.

"Laughlin, I need to talk to you about something. It has been bothering me since our walk home from the restaurant last night."

Laughlin had just placed our order and was pouring purified water from a glass jar. I needed to know if this was a fun affair, to last only days or weeks, or something else. If we were parting sooner rather than later, I needed the time to prepare my reset button.

Before I met him a few days ago, I'd been in love with my life and being single. Now, the idea of never seeing him again hurt my heart. Picturing my life before this trip was like taking swimming lessons in preparation for a cruise. My path had changed, and I needed to follow this and see where it led, even though I was treading a dangerous path.

"I know you've been chewing on something. Spill."

I smiled at his easy manner and was thankful for this aspect of his personality. I took a deep breath, knowing it was now or never. "I'm scheduled to fly home the day after we return to Selimiye."

His eyebrows rose slightly as if I had stated the obvious.

"Okay, I'm just going to say it, and all I ask for in return is honesty. Upon our return, are we done and over? I'm okay if that is the case, as I don't hold any expectations. To be completely honest, I need to guard my heart as you would be an easy man to fall for, and I need to prepare for the inevitable."

Laughlin appraised me, his eyes hooded and giving

nothing away as to his thoughts. "How would you like this to play out, Suri? If you're asking me if I'm having fun, then the answer is yes. I am having more fun than I have had in a very long time. Do I want it to continue with you when your time in Turkey is over? Yes, I would, but I don't know what else I can give you."

What was he saying? That this was as far as we would ever get? I was about to ask for clarification when he continued.

"I see you are confused; allow me to clarify. I have never been in a relationship and have, in fact, avoided them at all costs. I usually pay for sex when I want it, as there are no complications and I remain unburdened by commitment. I am a very singular man in my tastes, of which you've had a small sampling. When it comes to pleasure, Suri, we've barely begun to scratch that surface."

When he said pleasure, his pupils dilated, and the inflection in his tone changed. I found my lady parts squeezing in response.

"I like to control things; I like to deliver pleasure. I won't commit to anything, but I also don't want you to go. If you are agreeable, I would like you to continue with me. I have to go to Greece next and then back to Scotland. Would you like to come with me?"

Not what I expected, but I appreciated his honesty. "Can I think about it? I will let you know when we get back."

He nodded. "Of course, take your time."

I wasn't sure, but I think my answer surprised him. Had he expected me to fall all over myself in an attempt to keep him?

The Blue Mosque, not its original name, of course, but commonly referred to that now, was incredible. The construction began in sixteen hundred and nine and finished sometime in sixteen hundred and sixteen and contained over twenty thousand handmade tiles and stained glass.

We spent hours going through it and then attended the

Arasta Bazaar, located behind the mosque. It was a stellar bazaar, with finely made souvenirs and superb shopping. We were having so much fun, laughing and trying on funny hats and clothing. The music was loud and playful, lending to the holiday atmosphere that one felt immediately passing through its gates.

Not being a *stuff* person, I passed many stalls. But when I saw something I liked, Laughlin, ever attentive, purchased it. As I didn't have money issues, I didn't have purchasing issues. I discovered that one of the ways Laughlin gave and received pleasure was through gift-giving.

We finally had to leave the bazaar, as our arms were laden with cloth bags.

"Let's get a cab, Suri. It's a long walk in the heat with all of these packages."

"Good idea; I'm feeling a little overheated."

"Are you?" His eyes sparkled. "I know just the thing." We were barely in the door of our room when Laughlin began undressing me. Then he opened the drapes he'd kept closed when we checked in, saying it would help keep out the after-noon heat.

But really, he was hiding the best part of the suite, the deck with the private lap pool and hot tub. "Oh, wow, that looks like fun."

"My thoughts exactly," Laughlin responded, scooping me up in his arms and jumping into the deep end.

The cool water felt amazing on my heated skin. Laughlin dropped his mouth to mine, delivering a kiss that sent quivers down to my lady parts. Placing me in the shade at the edge of the pool, he parted my legs, then he delved his cool fingers into my hot core, parting my petals and dipping down to taste my nectar.

"Oh, god, yes."

Laughlin swirled his tongue around my hardening nub, his

strokes eliciting shivers down my spine, causing my walls to clench and unclench. He pressed two fingers inside me, his big hands having no problem hitting my G-spot while he continued to lick and suck my bud. I was going out of my mind with the intense sensations.

I was about to unleash a torrent when he slid a finger into my unsuspecting puckered hole. *What?* He pressed in and out, loosening the tight ring of muscle.

Now, as he moved both sets of fingers in and out simultaneously, I could feel his fingers through the thin wall that separated the two. Using his tongue, he pressed down on my nub, and I was done for. Fireworks went off as I unleashed my essence, drenching his fingers and tongue. He kept going, not letting up on his pace. I climaxed so many times, I thought I would pass out from pleasure. Then he abruptly stopped, drew me back into the water and carried me over to the stairs.

"On your knees, my gorgeous nymph."

I didn't need to be told twice. I loved what he'd done to me, but I also needed to feel him inside me. As soon as Laughlin entered me from a wheelbarrow position, I came undone. Anyone out on their decks would have heard me keening, screaming, and begging, all the while my responses spurring Laughlin to plunder deeply and thoroughly.

When he knew I couldn't possibly take any more, he had me sit on the stairs, and he stood in front of me, his large package in my direct eye line. I looked up at him, licking my lips. Dare I? Deciding to take some control. I implored him with innocent eyes, "What would you like, Sir?"

His hands immediately wound through my hair. "Open for me, beautiful woman; take my cock in your mouth." I had, in the past, engaged in using my mouth to bring a man to climax. But I had usually disassociated from the act. Being here with Laughlin, whom I craved with every fiber of my being, was a totally different experience.

I wanted to make him weak in the knees like he had done to me. I desired to milk his release from him like he'd done to me. I wanted to own his responses like he had with me. Using both hands, I encompassed his length.

I began to gently pump as I dipped my tongue to his tip, tasting his salty seed. It was difficult to hold back, as he was gripping my hair, and I wanted to enthusiastically take him deep in my throat, something I had never given much thought to before.

I stayed the course, Laughlin giving up all semblance of control, leaning back against the pool's edge. Now that I had the freedom to move as I liked, I licked and flicked and took him intensely, cupping his balls and running spirals over the puckered skin with my nails.

Laughlin was responsive, so much so that it was hard not to giggle at what the neighbors must be imagining. I could feel him tensing, getting closer to his release. With one hand pumping, I took him as deeply as I could, softening my throat.

Laughlin's hips began to thrust wildly, gaining control once again by wrapping his hand in my hair and holding me still. I ran my nails gently up his inner thighs, and he came with a roar, pumping down my throat, his head thrown back in ecstasy.

When his breathing slowed, he gazed down at me with an unreadable look. "Lass, that was the best I've ever had. Thank you for your gift." Wow, a man thanked me for returning the pleasure that he delivered to me so selflessly.

Laughlin pulled some flotation mats into the pool, and we climbed aboard, relaxing in what remained of the light. I closed my eyes and drifted, more relaxed than I'd ever been. When Laughlin roused me, it was time to shower and ready ourselves for dinner.

"I could lie here all night; do we really have to go for dinner?" I could tell that he was a little disappointed by my comment, and I wondered if he had booked something special. "On second thought, I am rather hungry after that workout. I'll go shower."

Laughlin beamed. Clearly, I'd made the right decision. Being a simple woman, I'd purchased items from the market that fit my personality. I exited the bathroom half an hour later, in sandals and a long, light linen dress with a plunging V-neckline and dual slits up the sides the length of my legs. It looked like it was made for me and I was quite happy with it.

Laughlin was in black slacks of some unknown light material and a tight black t-shirt that showed off his body. I was taken aback; the simpler he dressed, the more gorgeous he appeared. I wondered if the lord dressed so commonly back home.

"You look beautiful, Suri. That dress you chose is perfect."

"Thank you, my milord." I did a little curtsy.

Fifteen minutes later, we sat on 16 Roof, with a bird's eye view of the beautiful Sea of Marmara.

Chapter 8

Laughlin

We were currently on the beautiful island of Koufonisia, off the island of Crete, my next stop before heading back to Scotland. Marc, Sophie, and the other Templars were here as well. Our mission was to check into the rumors of an ancient stronghold once belonging to the Templar Knights.

Of course, Suri still remained ignorant as to the real reason for my trip. My investigations were proving frustrating. I still did not believe that what happened at the beach in Turkey was by accident. My gut told me that my inquiries were being hampered, but it was still a mystery who was spearheading the block.

Marc agreed with me regarding Suri's appearance in Turkey, while I was sure it was not an accident. I wanted to talk to her friend Tino, who was now back in New York. However, he'd gone off the grid, and again, my gut told me this was no coincidence.

Suri had an enviable capacity for living in the now, for

which I was thankful. Her near-death experience in Turkey was already a thing of the past.

I was just returned from a late meeting with the other Grand Masters to find no Suri. I quickly went to my suitcase and pulled out my gun, stalking through our beach bungalow, finally finding a note in the kitchen saying that she had gone for a swim.

Damn woman, I had asked her not to do these late-night jaunts when I wasn't around just in case, but she had laughed, in that gentle bell tinkling sound of hers. It was late, well past midnight, and the moon was only a crescent high in the sky.

I gazed in the water, looking for her, then scanned the beach. I spotted her as she emerged from the sea with glistening droplets streaming from her wet, naked body. She sat down on a towel cross-legged. I was about to call out when I caught a glimpse of two guys sneaking toward the newly named moon goddess. Hoping to catch the two, I took off my shoes and made my way towards her, keeping in the darkness of the bungalows that shadowed this end of the beach. The two men continued to sneak towards Suri, who seemed utterly oblivious to their presence.

I was only a few feet away now and could see that one carried a gun. "Stop right there!" The two spun around, and as they did, I dropped to my knees. The gunfire rang out loudly in the quiet of the night.

I shot back, hitting one, while the other took off. I chased the one running away, but not before stopping to retrieve the gun dropped by the assailant I'd shot. I chased the other assailant down the beach until he jumped into a car parked by the pier.

No longer able to carry on the chase, I ran back to Suri, to find her kneeling beside the man on the sand. She was gently swaying as she chanted some gibberish in a tongue I didn't recognize. Her hands were extended over the man with the gunshot wound. What the hell was she doing?

"Suri, what the hell are you doing? Get away from that guy."

She glanced up at me, and I noticed her eyes were different, deeper in color. "Call the ambulance, Laughlin. I will try to keep him alive as long as I can."

She was crazy. His life was worth nothing, but the fact that, once again, hers came close to ending and she seemed completely unaffected by it put me in a rage.

I leaned down over the guy on the sand. His eyes were closed, his breath shallow, and he had blood seeping from the corners of his mouth. I'd hit his lung. He wouldn't survive this, no matter what kind of energy she used.

I reached past her and grabbed his shirt. His eyes flew open at my abrupt mishandling. "Who the hell do you work for? Tell me, and I'll call an ambulance." The cocksucker had the nerve to smile at me. Then he stopped breathing and was dead a moment later.

I pulled out my phone and called Marc. "Can you get the cleanup crew down to my location? Suri had another attack, and I have one dead, about three hundred feet from my bungalow. Yes, she's fine for now." I glared at Suri as I issued a few more commands and then hung up the phone.

"Suri, inside, now!"

"Laughlin," she began.

"Get going. Now." She left, and I gathered up anything that could be connected to her or me. The cleaning crew we had on standby at every location would take care of the bullet. When I got back, I heard the shower. It was just as well, as I wasn't sure I could hold back my anger if she was standing in front of me right now. Maybe it was time for me to tell her the truth about what was really going on and how much danger she was in.

I entered the bedroom and sat on the bed, waiting for her. When she emerged from the bathroom, she quickly donned one of my large t-shirts and no undies. One less item for me to remove when I tipped her over my knee for a much-deserved lesson.

"Would you like to tell me what you were doing?"

"Channeling, I like to call it the God power. It is a funneling of an abundance of energy that lives within and around us all the time. All I did was learn how to harness it and channel it. As people refer to it as a *gift*, some say a *curse*, and I give it away to my fellow planet dwellers for free."

I was astounded. "I think you misunderstand what I am asking you, Suri. I was abundantly clear when I requested you stay inside while I was gone, and you agreed. I found you outside, being stalked by two assailants, one with a gun. If you think they were seeking you out for your energy, I can assure you, they were not."

She gulped, realizing now what I was saying. "I've told you that I am a dominant man. I told you I get my way, and when I tell you something, I expect my directions to be followed, don't I?"

She opened her mouth to speak, and I interrupted her. "Unless you are going to say yes, Sir, I suggest you don't speak. You're in enough trouble as it is."

She snapped her mouth closed but glared at me in defiance. At this rate, she would be dead long before we set foot in Scotland. I needed to make clear who was in charge and get control of the situation. Despite my desire to hold and comfort her, I needed to stay firm.

My phone pinged with a message. One of our crew members had removed all evidence, and they would run the guy's prints back at our temporary headquarters and let me know, when I went in for a briefing the next day, what they'd managed to learn about the identity of the perp.

I quickly typed back a cursory response and then turned off my phone. "Look at me, Suri." Her eyes quickly moved to mine. "Do you remember when I spanked you in Turkey because you were rude?"

She nodded.

I raised my eyebrows at her.

"Yes, Sir." Her verbal acknowledgment came out with barely constrained anger. One thing I'd learned about Suri, she was a total brat. All of her. *I've let go of earthly connections and only seek the divine* was bull crap for the most part.

I was neither a wimp like her boyfriends, nor was I a manipulative ass like her ex-husband. No, I was neither of those, and it was time she learned that through a painful lesson. Ultimately, if she continued to shrug me off and disregard her word, there was no possibility of us remaining together.

"This will be a lot worse than that." Her eyes widened in surprise. I think she thought I was joking, but by my resolute expression, she realized her mistake. "Come here, over my knee."

Suri's face became a battleground of expressions, her anger morphing into a pout, stoicism, embarrassment and finally, guilt. That told me all I needed to know regarding my next steps. Suri, I suspected, still beat herself up over her choices before moving to New York. She had so many vibrant aspects to her personality. Why she continued to get caught up on her choices was beyond me. Then as I continued to stare her down, I saw something I had missed—the insecurity.

She needed my particular brand of discipline, to restore her and let her know she was okay. I tipped her over my lap and wrapped one of my large legs over her smaller ones, securing her in place. She would wiggle, and I didn't want to spank anything I shouldn't. I have huge hands and used them to my advantage, taking both her wrists in one.

"Suri, tell me why you're over my lap." She stayed resolutely silent. I brought my hand down on her backside hard. She let out a small screech. Oh yes, my bratty siren, there would be no warm-up. I was all in and ready to deliver a proper lesson. The first twenty spanks can be the absolute worst when there is no warm-up, Suri proving my point by screeching like a banshee and doing her best to kick her legs. Her cool, soft skin quickly changing to an angry red.

I suspected that being as expressive as she was, she sounded much worse than she should and was probably adding in the drama to make me feel guilty and pity her. But in the almost two weeks we'd been together, I'd fallen hard for this woman, and I wasn't going to let her die on my watch, and if that meant a sound spanking, then so be it.

After I unleashed forty on her backside, I took a break. Suri hung limply over my lap, sniveling and drawing in gulps of air. She wasn't crying yet, and her posture still held defiance.

"Suri, why are you over my lap?"

"Because." She sniffed. "You are a tyrant, and I hate you." It was all I could do to not laugh—what a paradox she was, so free-spirited and loving and independent and then totally bratty.

"Well, I don't hate you, love." I picked up my antique wooden hairbrush, made from solid oak, and picked up where I left off, holding nothing back. She would be very sore, but it would be worth it if she remained alive.

When Suri hung over my lap, bawling her eyes out and begging for forgiveness, I knew my work had paid off. I pulled her up and held her tight. This wasn't something I had ever done before. When you paid for fun, there was no aftercare, except payment. I found myself treading in new waters.

"I'm sorry, Laughlin, I won't break my word again. I promise."

I looked her dead in the eye. "Oh, lass, don't make promises you can't keep." She looked shocked, then we both burst out in laughter, the tension melting away. "Lie on the bed on your tummy. I want to admire my handiwork."

"Oh, you," she said, blushing prettily with not a hint of anger in her eyes. She climbed onto the bed and lay on her belly. Her ass was scarlet and turning blue in her sit spots.

Good; she would feel that every time she sat down for the next week.

I gently squeezed her backside, and she squealed at first touch, but as I continued to gently knead her burning skin, Suri began to buck her hips, opening her legs wider. I pulled her to her knees and dipped my head down to taste her.

Her silky folds were drenched and her nub already hard and needy. I swirled my tongue and inserted one of my fingers. Suri let out a moan that almost sounded like a growl. I was taking her to a new edge, and her primal self was quickly taking over. The little minx had gotten the hardest spanking I'd ever delivered, and still, she was wet for me.

I curled my finger and began to pump. Suri's nerves were so stimulated already that two pumps were all it took for her sheath to convulse and release. Her essence soaked my hand with her release and was accompanied by a primal scream.

Suri writhed on the bed with need. She was utterly unleashed, needing all I could give. I pulled her knees to the end of the bed, shoved my finger in and took her with my digit, while I used my other hand to lightly spank her reddened backside. She was moaning and writhing and bucking her hips as her next release carried on with no end before she convulsed and tipped over the edge again.

This went on for long minutes until her bucking calmed down to gentle undulations. Needing to be inside her warmth, I undid my pants and plunged into her quivering junction. She screeched like a banshee and immediately started pressing back into my aggressive strokes. Every time I collided into her backside, she mewled with need.

I knew the sensations I created were stimulating her nerve endings, and when I hit this sensitive area, it would throw her off the edge. Her walls never unclenched, staying in a state of hyper response and milking my cock in a way I'd never experienced.

At this rate, I would be unloading in seconds. I reached down and pressed that glorious button of hers and felt her come apart. If I hadn't been holding her, she would have collapsed as she spasmed around my cock. I howled like a wolf as I unleashed a torrent with an intensity never before felt.

When I came down, Suri was still panting, and the moment I released her, she fell forward on the bed.

"Oh my god." Her words were muffled by the blanket. "Laughlin, that was crazy! Never have I ever felt anything so, so, cosmic."

I chuckled. My crazy Reiki yoga girl was back. Cosmic indeed, but I had to agree, sex with Suri was out of this world.

Chapter 9

Suri

I t had been three days since that awful spanking Laughlin had delivered. My ass was still swollen, and it hurt to sit down. Laughlin seemed intent on reminding me of my lesson, often pulling me onto his lap where I would land with a *thunk* and a groan. Even now, he was across the room staring at me, with that same look he'd had when he'd taken me across his lap.

"Come on, you giant Scotsman, stop dreaming of my ass and let's go." He smiled and chugged down the rest of his wine. "No need to tell me twice, lass. I was just noticing that your ass looks a little bigger than the last time you wore that red dress." He smirked as if daring me to challenge him so he could give me the lesson again.

I had to admit, as painful as it was, the heat had gone to all the right places and our sex had been mind-blowing. I returned Laughlin's smile with a curtsey. "It is a temporary change, my lord. You were thinking of this dress today, were you not? I figured it was time to wear it again."

"How the bloody hell? Are you a mind reader now?"

I smiled. "No, but I know you, Laughlin, and your thoughts and desires are not hidden from me. I did put it on my dating application, didn't I?"

He laughed. "You did indeed, now let's get going, no doubt Marc and Sophie are waiting for us."

As we walked home a few hours later, I was more talkative than usual. Over-stimulated was a better term, like a kid who played too many video games. "Laughlin, wasn't the food fantastic? The scallops were so buttery, they melted in my mouth. And the wine, mmm, what a great pairing. What a lovely evening."

Beside me, Laughlin chuckled at my enthusiasm "Yes, everything was delightful, and you were full of funny anecdotes tonight. It's a good thing you and Marc steered the conversation, as poor Sophie was lost during most of our talk. I can't believe she thought the Big Bopper was a hamburger. I have not spent a lot of time in the Americas, but I certainly know who the Big Bopper was. Chantilly Lace even reached us over here in Scotland. Mind you, I wasn't alive yet, but my father played records that my mother had enjoyed as a young girl."

"Actually, I kind of understood. Sophie is only twenty-two? Why would she know a singer from the 1950s? The one that I found amusing was her inability to understand time change. It is a North American thing, and she is from L.A."

"True, true... so where was your head, lass, when Marc graciously did the ordering for us, yet again?"

I did not give an immediate answer, taking a moment to formulate a response that accurately relayed my musings. "Honestly, I was using the four of us as comparisons to identity, career, and perception. I find the duality of difference and sameness fascinating, and you and Marc provided the perfect backdrop to my thinking."

"Oh? How so?"

"Neither of you fit the general acceptance of what lords look like, and certainly not nerdy ones who fund climate change projects. Neither of you fit, yet you are both so completely different from each other as well. A true anomaly."

"Mmm, that is an interesting perception. Suri…" Laughlin seemed as if he wanted to say more, but he remained silent as we entered our beach bungalow. He checked things out to ensure no one had broken in while we were gone, then went to the fridge and pulled out a bottle of Gerovassiliou Avaton and two bottles of water.

"You didn't mention you and Sophie. You aren't that far off in age."

I laughed at the idea of comparisons of Sophie and me. "Age maybe, but everything else, well, I feel we are worlds apart. I am twenty-six, a widow, and a freedom seeker with very little desire for material wealth, preferring experiences over things."

I took off my shoes and sat on the overstuffed chair facing him.

His mien seemed grim as he handed me a glass of wine and a bottle of water. Kicking off his shoes, he sat on the couch facing me. "I wanted to tell you something you may feel is vital about the night those two men snuck up on you at the beach. Please remember that regardless of what I now share, I am still the same man. This new information changes nothing about me or what exists between us."

I took a gulp of water and waited for him to continue. I was finally getting some answers, and no way would I ruin the moment. Keeping my face as blank as possible, I nodded for him to continue.

"I am very interested in the environment, and I am a nerdy environmentalist, as you have stated. Marc and I are part of the Templars, known more commonly now as the Masons, or Freemasons."

I gazed expectantly, as his confession had zero impact on me. Wasn't that a glorified men's club these days?

"You don't know what those are, do you?"

I sighed, sitting up a little straighter. "I am vaguely aware. My father belongs to a club like that. I just assumed it was a men's club, an excuse to get away from the wife and drink expensive scotch."

Laughlin smiled, but it did not reach his eyes. "We have certainly worked hard on sharing that idea with the world. After all, the more clubbish it sounds, the fewer eyebrows raised. Anyway, I am a Grand Master, and I meet with the other Grand Masters a few times per year to discuss issues. Marc is my right-hand man and next in line to be a Grand Master."

Laughlin appeared disconcerted by my lack of response to his confession, but he continued. "I was in Turkey investigating my father's death. It wasn't an accident. We modern Templars can be described as many things, one of which is an assassin. We have been trained in martial and military arts. In fact, my entire early education was completely devoted to learning the role I would one day step into."

"So those men on the beach may have been after you and not me?" I was a little irritated, thinking I'd endured that horrible spanking for nothing. Then I remembered that it wasn't about what he told me, but that I'd given my word and broke it. I felt the familiar flush of embarrassment creep up my cheeks.

"No, Suri, they were definitely after you. But as to why, we still don't know that. We ran a background check on the man who died on the beach. He had several identities, and we recognized one as a spy for the French underground in Lyon. They have been after the Templar treasure since 1314, when they burned alive our first Grand Master, Jacques de Molay, in Paris."

"Holy crap!"

Laughlin nodded his head sagely.

"Spain, France, and England have been trying to get their hands on the treasure. Historically, many of our members have been caught, tortured and murdered. In the current political climate, it is challenging for a prestigious member of the realm to just disappear. Disappearances have been few, our enemies selective. That is why going after you didn't make sense."

"But I thought you said those two men were from Turkey, that they had seen me and wanted to shut my mouth, indefinitely."

"That is true, Suri, but the crime you stumbled upon was a member of Knights Templar, low on the scale of the hierarchy, but a historian who they probably felt could give them locations of secret bunkers."

"Bunkers?"

"A conversation for another time but know he has been found and relocated for his own safety." Now I realized the seriousness of that simple act in Turkey and what it had cost me. I was known to the French mafia and their affiliates. They would gun for me even though I knew nothing.

"There is one other matter. I am unclear at this point if it is related, but you said you are a Sinclair on your mothers' side." I nodded in affirmation.

"The Sinclairs are part of the Templars' history. Have either of your parents shared anything about your past?"

I thought back. Was there anything that would give away that they might be part of a secret organization? "No." I shook my head. "My father has a locked drawer in his desk in his office back home. I know he has a safe as well, but I have never overheard anything that would make me think he was part of a secret organization. But then, I didn't pick that up with you, either." I laughed at the irony.

Laughlin's eyes were intense, like he was digging for the truth. I had nothing to hide, but I did believe that nothing happened by accident, so I could understand his reservation in hearing my denial of knowledge of a secret sect.

"Um, so, the guys on the beach were connected to the mafia?"

"Yes, the one we identified is a known member of a sect of the French mafia known as SOG, Servants of God, a resistance militia who are descendants of the Catholic Church and worked to annihilate the Templars. Next to us, they are the premier authorities on Templar history." What Laughlin was saying was beginning to make sense.

"Okay, so was it divine timing that had you and your group of masters in the same town in Turkey, where another person was being held for information on secrets that you guys have? I mean, that can't be a coincidence. And if so, why not attack the group, why him?"

Laughlin laughed. "I love your desire for the truth, Suri. Most women would have run screaming, never to return. But here you are, digging for the truth. You are an uncommon woman."

That I was, and I appreciated that he could see it in me, just another reason to fall in love with this puzzling man.

"In answer to your question, our man lives in Turkey. It could be a coincidence that he was captured when we had our meeting. We are still trying to understand that ourselves. Marc wondered if they used our historian as bait. Or, if maybe you were meant to be the bait that pulled us out of our safe zone."

A feeling of fear, with the onslaught, overcame me. This was an issue I had not yet learned to overcome. I told Laughlin that first night that I meditated when I needed to work through difficult things, and now was one of those times. "I need to go outside and meditate."

Laughlin's eyes became steel, "No, Suri, it's not safe."

Something inside of me snapped, born out of desperation and not reality, and the brat in me roared to life. "Then I'm leaving. That's it; I am done with being told what I can and cannot do. I lived with an asshole who held me back, and I won't do it again, no matter how good the sex is!"

Laughlin stalked towards me, his primal energy sending off shockwaves in my body. I ran from the living room, like a deer from a cougar, and reached the sliding door, just as Laughlin wrapped his large arm around my waist.

He lifted me easily and carried me to the bedroom while I kicked and screamed. "I hate you, Laughlin Campbell, Earl of who gives a crap. Put me down!"

Laughlin dumped me on the bed, crawling on top of me and using his great size and strength to hold me down. "I am not that man, Suri, so stop painting me as your ex when you become fearful or overwrought."

Damn him, for chipping away at my armor. Sure, he could be my safety net while we were together, but then what? Inevitably, we would part, and then I would be back to learning to self-govern again. I couldn't allow myself this weakness.

Laughlin leaned in and planted soft kisses from my ear to my throat while the anger I'd felt so intensely, only moments ago, deflated and quickly morphed into passion. Laughlin continued to drop sensual kisses towards my breasts. My body betrayed me and arched up to meet him. We'd had sex hours earlier. How could one ache again so quickly?

Laughlin slid my dress up and kneed my legs apart. He suckled and nipped at my hardening buds. I groaned, thrusting towards his hot mouth. His laving and cooling breath igniting a fire that spread down to my core.

My anger and passion fused, creating a raw, primal being. I thrust maniacally beneath Laughlin while he continued to play with my nipples. The heat continued to build and brew deep inside me. Just when I thought I couldn't take any more, Laughlin stopped and drew up onto his knees then rolled me onto my shoulders and widened my knees so they dropped by my ears, and he plunged inside me.

I screeched with the intensity, immediately falling off the edge, into my first orgasm. The position I was in didn't allow me to return Laughlin's thrusts, so I focused on the sensations he was delivering.

I realized he had pinned me on purpose, and without control, I had to accept his pleasure. Taking away my ability to respond had been smart, as I was tuned in to him in a way I hadn't been so far. Laughlin's rod hit its mark with each stroke, and I found that my orgasms had no end and no beginning. My essence flowed, soaking us both. Then he pulled out and, using the position, placed his hard tip at the entrance of my puckered hole. I waited for the resistance, but Laughlin slid in and slowly impaled me. I really was in the perfect position for anal sex as I couldn't fight it, and for the first time, I indeed saw the pleasure this position provided.

When Laughlin was fully in, he began to slowly move. I moaned and wished for some interaction elsewhere. Reading my mind, he pressed down on my clit, and again, the fireworks went off, driving me off the edge.

I moaned and grunted in time to his anal assault, which was taking me to new heights of pleasure. "Laughlin, I need to change position."

He stayed inside me and slowly brought down my legs. The full feeling changed as the pressure alleviated. But he wasn't done. Slowly, Laughlin turned me until I was on my knees. The twisting sensation was unbelievable, so intense.

When he had fully rotated us, he reached between my knees and gently patted my bud.

I erupted with the impact. He took my behind hard and fast now, and I lost my mind in sensation, literally a quivering mess. I could feel the even strokes and the increasing girth of his cock as he readied for his own release. As he roared, he set off one more fire deep in me, and I keened with my orgasm.

Unable to stay on my knees any longer, I flopped forward and stayed there, unmoving. The anger and need for meditation were gone. As I lay there, I took in gulps of air and realized that there was more than one way to center oneself, and this new way was the best of all.

Chapter 10

Laughlin

S uri was proving to be my biggest challenge. She was unlike any woman I had ever met before. Giving myself to her, proclaiming my love for her, should be an easy feat. But my one college experience had left a foul taste in my mouth for intimacy.

We'd arrived in Scotland the previous evening, and immediately, I felt better. My estate was very secure, and I didn't have to worry as much about Suri's safety. When she'd seen the pool lagoon with the sand bottom, a huge smile had filled her face.

"I guess I know where to find you if you disappear again," I'd said playfully. Suri had blushed prettily.

Now that we were back home and I had access to my global computer spy network complete with encrypted coding, I could do uncensored digging into what had happened in Turkey and Greece. But first, I promised the lass a tour of the Edinburgh marketplace.

The event was a glorified farmers' market, nothing special

like the Blue Mosque. But Suri, having never been to Scotland, wanted to immerse herself in the culture, and the market would be an excellent place to start.

Today, I was just Laughlin, not Duke or Earl, and to dress the part, I was in a pair of faded blue jeans and a white t-shirt. I wore sunglasses, and I thought looked inconspicuous. Suri descended the staircase in a barely-there halter and short shorts. She must have noticed my eyes bugging out, because a Cheshire grin immediately lighted her face.

"No, Suri, just no. You said you wanted to be anonymous. I can tell you, lass, that you are anything but in that."

A tinkling of bells let loose from her beautiful mouth. "Are you sure?" she husked. "I thought this outfit would remind you all day long what you have to come home to."

"Oh, well, it does that, and probably a hundred other men who will follow us home. Please change."

Another tinkling of bells as she whirled around, only to return five minutes later, matching me in jeans and a non-descript t-shirt and carrying a large, gypsy-looking basket bag that she said was for her purchases.

As I watched her walk down the staircase, I had a flash of her in a formal gown, coming down to meet our guests. The image was lost almost immediately, but it left a lasting impression. I could host a party for the higher echelons of Scottish society.

"Hello, handsome. I'm ready."

"So I see, and you look lovely."

"Laughlin, how can I possibly look lovely wearing jeans and a t-shirt?"

I pressed her up against the door, dipped my head, and drank in her luscious lips, taking a moment to plunder her beautiful mouth. When I let her up for air, her pupils were dilated. I loved that her appetite for bedroom fitness was as lusty as my own. But we had a market to get to, or I would have scooped her up and taken her back upstairs.

As Suri gazed up at me with a look of complete devotion, I felt my insides freeze in fear. I wasn't ready for that type of relationship, no matter how lovely it would be. Getting over what happened in college seemed beyond me. "Well, your fine arse looks good in anything," I responded, to lighten the mood.

I tugged her out the door and into the car. Suri took notice of the Sinclair emblem as we were passing through the property's gates. "Laughlin, how is it you are a Campbell but own a castle and estate that once belonged to the Sinclairs?"

"That, lass, is a tale of intrigue, taking more time than our short drive into Edinburgh. However, to put it plainly, the original owner William Sinclair, first Earl of Roswell, had a few wives. Those wives produced several sons."

Beside me, Suri giggled. "Quite prolific, I guess."

"That they were. To continue, the eldest son inherits the domains, and the lesser or following sons receive smaller pieces or go off to war or find some other way to make their way in the world. In any case, our family lands were divided, and more than once. It wasn't until my grandfather inherited that all of the holdings came back under one owner."

Suri seemed thoughtful. "I guess that was a strategic marriage. Was there any love between them?"

That was a good question, and one to which I didn't know the answer. "I can't say. I never knew them or my mother. Everyone seems to die mysteriously in my family. My father was very active in my life and encouraging, but I wouldn't say he ever acted lovingly, so if that indicates his parents, then I would have to say not."

We were cresting the outskirts of the old town and wanted to bring our conversation to an end. Talking about my family with anyone made me very uncomfortable, because there was not much to share.

"Because of whom my grandfather married, a descendant from the second family, in essence, my father became the sole inheritor of Roswell and brought all titles and holdings into one fold, of which I am currently the head."

I pulled into a vacant spot and turned off the car.

"It must be lonely." Suri was gazing at me with that look again.

I felt sweat break out on my skin. "Not really. I was created for it, so it fits like a glove."

Suri's gaze looked mildly hurt by my acerbic response.

Afraid I would say anything more, I quickly exited the car, and when I opened her door, my façade was safely planted on my face. "Come, moon goddess, let me guide thy fair lady to her shopping." She took my hand, and I led her to the market.

I looked around, stunned. The Edinburgh market had grown since I'd attended as a boy. There were artisans and even fortunetellers and healing art booths that had not been here when last I visited.

Suri squealed with delight as we made our way through the main gate. "Laughlin, this is awesome. I feel like I have found my people."

I smiled at her enthusiasm. She did seem like she was in her element, but I think Suri was still selling herself short. She seemed like she was comfortable everywhere we went together. People genuinely responded to her, including me. I watched as she stopped and chatted to a vendor and talked as if they were old friends. I remembered my father saying that back in his day, my mother had been similar. People flocked to her, he'd said. The only time I'd seen the old man with real emotion in his eyes was when he spoke of my mother.

I was drawn from my thoughts by Suri's tinkling laughter. I glanced to see what she had found so amusing, only to find her in a flirtatious discussion with a handsome young man. She was at the artisan cheese stand, and the guy was probably nineteen or twenty years old.

His eyes shone with the attention that Suri gave to him, and I could tell he had fallen quite smitten with her. The little minx sashayed away from the stand, giving the guy a good eyeful of her perfect ass. I was about ready to go and bust his face in for looking at her like that. But as Suri neared, she winked at me. What the devil?

When she was in proximity of my long arms, I reached and pulled her to me possessively and squeezed her ass. She placed one hand behind my neck, pulling my mouth down to hers, and allowed me to pillage her mouth. I squeezed her ass hard as I continued to possess her mouth.

I could feel her melting into me, her breath hitching. She did this on purpose. I would have to teach her a lesson later. It was hard to not laugh when she finally pulled away, and we both glanced to the guy in the booth whose cheeks were now red with embarrassment, and his jaw hung, slightly ajar.

"You are such a brat, lass."

Suri burst out in good-natured laugher as we waltzed away. " Sorry, Loc, I couldn't help it. He was so obviously trying to pick me up, I had to have a little fun with it."

My eyes glinted, but I said nothing, already thinking of our playtime later that night. She didn't know it yet, but Suri was going to meet the other side of Laughlin, the dark side.

Chapter 11

Suri

Laughlin's vacant veneer went south as he watched me interact with cheese boy. How glorious to see his look of possessive dominance rear its head. I knew how he felt about me. It was he who was in denial about it.

As we moved through the market, I felt invigorated by my shenanigans. Yes, I was acting a little bratty and knew Laughlin was plotting out my demise for later that night. The 'lost in thought' look accompanied by glinting eyes was a tell-tale sign.

What was funny about our dynamic was he thought I didn't know who he was or what he was. I didn't give away anything and just allowed him to unveil himself at his pace. I was in no rush for anything to change between us, as Laughlin seemed to be fighting with a demon he needed to be rid of.

I understood that, as I had experienced something similar. It was hard to carry such a burden, and in knowing that, I was at peace with our relationship as it was. " Laughlin, let's go to the tarot reader booth."

He rolled his eyes at me. "Really, Suri, it's all rubbish."

"Well, if it's all rubbish, then you won't mind a reading, and besides, I've always wanted to try." I took his hand and steered him over to Madame Kasa's booth. An older lady was just leaving, and I wanted to get there so we wouldn't have to wait in line, something I was sure Laughlin wouldn't do. The man owned his world and waited for no one.

Madame Kasa gazed up at me and smiled warmly. Her gaze then traveled farther up, almost comically so, to Laughlin's face. Her eyes narrowed, and her smile altered to a tight grimace.

"Sit," she commanded Laughlin, who had been gazing curiously at Madame Kasa. Seconds seemed like minutes, as Laughlin stood staring at the woman who ran the stand. Finally sitting, Madame Kasa wasted no time.

"Hold these cards in your left hand and begin to shuffle them, left to right. You will feel a pull, and three cards will jump from the pile. Place each one face down from left to right." Laughlin took the deck and placed it in his right hand. I was curious and leaned in to watch for the *jumping cards*. Laughlin was in his third shuffle when a card literally jumped from the deck, landing on the table. He continued, and three shuffles later, two cards jumped out together. Laughlin placed them down as he'd been instructed.

Madame Kasa turned over the first card and shifted her gaze to Laughlin. "You have been deceived by someone close to you. The betrayal has affected your life's course, and even now, you are seeking to rectify the situation."

Laughlin's expression remained impassive, giving nothing away to the card reader, neither denying or agreeing to what she said.

The second card was turned over by Madame Kasa, revealing a floating hand holding a chalice. There was water pouring from the chalice like a fountain. "You are in a new relationship." Madame Kasa glanced at me. "This relationship is pure, like the water flowing from the chalice; it indicates a chance at long-term love."

Laughlin didn't respond, keeping his face firmly set with no emotion.

Then Madame Kasa turned over the last card, and her face crinkled in consternation. It was a picture of a tower with people falling from it. I had never done a card reading myself, but I assumed this picture indicated disaster, as the people falling seemed afraid.

"Understand that your world will soon change. You will gain truths that will shake the foundations of your world, and it will feel like there is no hope. But the universe has given you a partner to help you through this tough time. Whether the partner is with you when the dust settles, I do not know. There is a chance she may be, and there is a chance that she will not. Who she is, is not who she will be. And who you are, is not who you will be. You will both need to decide if being together serves your greater selves when the time comes."

Laughlin had still not said anything but stood, pulled out fifty pounds and placed it on the table. Gazing at Madame Kasa, he thanked her and, taking my hand, walked quickly from the stall.

When we were at least twenty feet away, I pulled us to a stop. "Laughlin, what is wrong? You seem very upset by what she read in your cards."

His face was set now in a resolute grimace as he took a deep breath and let it out slowly. "I believe my father was killed by someone close to home. For the longest time, I have been investigating his murder and coming up with nothing. I had hoped that Turkey would reveal his killers. But now I see what has been right under my nose this entire time."

"So, you think it is a Templar, someone here in Scotland?"

"No, lass, I believe it is worse than that. It is a family

member, someone wanting to remove my claim. It all makes sense to me now, the attack you witnessed and the one you almost fell victim to. You are a Sinclair, and I'll bet if I dug deep enough, I would find connections to my family."

"Are you saying it's my family's fault that your father was murdered?"

Laughlin seemed thoughtful. "No, I'm saying that someone in the line, someone who can benefit from having both of us out of the picture, planned everything. Did your family know where you were going for your holiday?"

"Only my sister. I haven't spoken to my parents since I shamed them publicly. Edward's misappropriations of funds made the news, and when he killed himself, I was blamed. My parents, who traveled in the same social circles as the Stanhopes, were socially ostracized."

Laughlin mulled this over. "We need to tread carefully, lass, as there seems to be more going on than meets the eye, and I don't know who to trust."

I shuddered and finally wondered if coming to Scotland with Laughlin was such a good idea.

"What now?"

"Well, we can't solve this mystery all in one day, so let's go enjoy the market, as planned."

I nodded, allowing him to lead me back into the growing crowd. But I couldn't enjoy it as I had earlier. I was included in a mystery I knew nothing about, and there was no turning back. I needed to know what was going on and if Laughlin and I would be standing in the end.

Chapter 12

Laughlin

"Geoff, it's good to hear your voice. Anything new in Canada?" Our Grand Master for our Canadian chapter had sent me an urgent message. It seemed things were heating up for the Order worldwide.

"We've had a few incidents of late, and we aren't the only ones. I am concerned that all of these small attacks on the Order is a sleight of hand trick." This was the first I was hearing of anything going on in Canada. More disconcerting was the information being blocked. It reminded me of my father's murder investigations. If I was only hearing about things now, how much worse was it on the ground?

"Geoff, I am beginning to wonder, myself, what is going on. Do you think this could be internal?" The line was silent as I waited for Geoff to organize his response to my question. Even with our secure network, if the threat was coming from inside the Order, we had to be careful.

"How's the weather in Scotland at this time of year?" So,

he was thinking the same thing, and our encrypted channels were not safe.

"Fantastic, it's about time you took my offer on that fishing trip I promised. How about this weekend?"

"That sounds like a plan, and I'll bring some of the boys. I know they miss Scotland and wouldn't want to miss out on the chance to catch a prize fish."

"That's great news, Geoff. We will see you on Saturday; text me your landing details, and I will have the car pick you up." Geoff hung up, and I moved around my desk to gaze outside. From here, I could see Suri in the distance, swimming in the lagoon.

I needed a plan in place and decided that until Geoff and I had time to discuss what was going on with the Masons, I would trust no one. Grabbing a burner phone, I placed a call to the head of my private security force.

"Thorsten, the world is a dangerous place, not because of those who do evil, but because of those who look on and do nothing." I waited to see if he would give me the correct response. By his vow, he couldn't give me the answer I needed if he wasn't real.

"Human's first attribute is courage; everything else is secondary." I breathed a sigh of relief.

"Thor, when can you be here? We need to discuss security."

"I'm on my way, sir, my ETA is fifteen." I hung up the phone and began to formulate a plan. Thorsten's father had been the head of my father's security, and he had been killed. Could I trust the son? His response said I could, but I still needed to tread carefully.

Unlike me, Geoff seemed to have a very dedicated team who would take a bullet for him. He inspired strong leadership in his team. I thought I could borrow some of his team for a short bit, as he brought the key players with him. Or, maybe by sharing my issues and needs with Geoff, another idea would be offered.

Ultimately, I felt like there was a pressure cooker, and it was getting ready to blow. When it did, I wanted the best in place. I wasn't worried about myself, as I had participated in organized fights worldwide and knew I was as deadly as they came. It was Suri's safety I wanted to ensure, until the threat was uncovered and we could move on.

That brought up another pressure cooker, of the relationship kind. Even if I wanted to, I couldn't let Suri go, for two reasons. She was in danger, and I felt responsible, and for another, she was part of the transformation the tower card revealed at the reading a week ago. I wanted Suri with me and when the tower inevitably fell, then we would decide if we had anything outside of this nefarious mystery to hold us together.

The sex was beyond anything I'd ever experienced before. I knew this was due to our intimacy and a willingness to try anything I suggested. I watched as Suri moved in the shallow end of the water, smoothly transitioning through yoga poses, her beautiful body glistening in the sunshine.

My cock stiffened at the sight of her. I had very little control these days over my body's response to her. I was working on letting go of the past and embracing a brave new future. It wasn't that simple. Of course, many things worked against me, but after researching PTSD, I realized I matched most of the criteria, based on the college experience—a situation that had rendered me helpless and utterly humiliated at the time.

With all I had witnessed, death and murder, one would think a simple experience from college days would weigh in low on the scale of atrocities to have nightmares about. But I did visualize my night with Theresa in my dreams… nightmares. Usually, after amazing scenes with Suri, it would often rear its ugly head. The repeated memory came with a physical component of gut pain, panic, and fear—serotonin overload.

The research proved that the warrior gene, monoamine oxidase A, was a front-runner for regulating serotonin levels from the fight or flight response and biofeedback. Being a hobby scientist, I knew a dozen practitioners in the biofeedback field. I lifted my phone and called Alice Malcolm, the most forthright woman I had ever met. Dedicated and passionate about helping others, she no longer had a practice, retiring young to explore myth and archetypes around the world.

"Well, if it isn't Scotland's most eligible bachelor."

I laughed at her frankness. "Hello, Alice, how are you?"

"Simply perfect, as always, but clearly you are not, or you wouldn't be calling me."

Alice and I were of the same age, and she had been in university when I was, having a first-hand account of the rumors that plagued me.

"I think you know why I'm calling. It's time to face my demons, Alice."

"I understand perfectly. When would you like to get started?"

That was an excellent question? I really didn't and wished this issue would disappear on its own but wishes never did what work could. I could go tomorrow, telling Suri that I had a meeting. "Tomorrow too soon?"

"See you then, Laughlin." Alice hung up on her end, and I was about to give in to my needs when Thorsten arrived.

"Have a seat, Thor."

I took a chair, and for the next hour, we discussed who was loyal and who was questionable. We increased security at the castle and personal protection for Suri when I wasn't with her. After creating a rotation schedule, we discussed the weekend with Geoff and his men.

Of course, Thor knew them all, and when I mentioned that they were coming, his face lit up. "It's been a while since the Canadians joined us. It will be quite a weekend."

"That it will. I will expect you to be included in all the festivities and meetings. You will be running everything for me on our end."

Thor nodded as he stood and shook my hand. "Thank you for giving me so much trust, Lord Roswell."

"Laughlin, please, and we are in this together, Thor. If anything comes up, anything at all, you will contact me."

He nodded his head, opening the door and going to the guard station to check in with our perimeter security.

Finally, I gave in to my needs and made my way out to the lagoon. Suri was lying on the edge of the water, stretching. I grabbed her extended leg and ran my hand down her calf.

Her glazed eyes peered up at me. "Just what I was dreaming about, a handsome rogue to take advantage of me."

That was all the invitation I needed. I stripped and walked into the lagoon in which I kept the temperature at twenty-six Celsius all spring and summer.

After a few laps, I walked towards Suri, who had been leaning on her elbows, watching me. A small smile curved her beautiful lips. Her mouth was an invitation, and I accepted it. Dropping down at her feet, I parted her legs.

She moaned, dropping her head back as I ran my tongue along her fragrant seam. She tasted of sweet nectar and the salt of the pool. I flicked her sensitive nub with my tongue and felt her body stiffen in anticipation.

Then, I rolled onto my back and turned her as I pulled her on top. Her beautiful petals were aligned over my mouth. I licked, and her back arched. Wanting to keep her nestled in tight, I gripped her gorgeous backside and held her still as her mouth descended over my cock.

"Och, Suri, your mouth is heaven." I had stopped licking to groan out my appreciation of her expert fellatio skills.

Her mouth pulled off my rod with a pop sound. "Your heavenly cock makes it easy, Loc."

I smiled at her calling my rod heavenly. As I felt her nearing her orgasm, I slid her off my mouth and sat her down on my cock, facing away. This angle would give her untold pleasure. She began to grind against me, her breath coming out in wanton pants.

"Oh, my God!" she cried as she went over the edge, her juices flowing over me.

We were on a gentle downward slope, and I used it to my advantage. Opening my legs, I had her put her hands on the sandy ground, slightly leaning forward, so I had a view of her rounded globes. I gripped her hips and, using my feet as leverage, began pounding into her. Within seconds, Suri was screaming out her second release. Watching that bouncing backside of hers, was an aphrodisiac that propelled me right over the edge.

———

The next day, I arrived at Alice's office. We met in a well-appointed room, with a beautiful antique desk in the center. The décor was an eclectic motif collection from her world travels. One could spend a few hours looking at everything stuffed onto the shelves.

"How can I help you, old friend?"

I sat back and sighed. Alice's familiar greeting was meant to put me at ease, and it worked. I wondered for the thousandth time if I should share the whole story or only what I felt affected my relationship with Suri.

Alice gave me a pointed look. "Start at the beginning."

I thought back, visualizing myself as a young nineteen-year-old with no experience at all with women. Inwardly, I rolled my eyes at how stupid I was. Surely, Alice would think me a complete idiot.

"I was a college freshman and nineteen years old. My experiences with females were limited. I had no sexual or dating experience beyond crushes and my right hand." I paused and looked Alice square in the eyes to see if there was any judgment.

Her eyes held steady as she nodded for me to continue.

"Obviously, I thought about women and hoped college would be an education in more than one way. As you no doubt heard at the time, I got a lot more than I bargained for. In my first year, I focused on general sciences. There were few women in my classes, and I thought I was doomed to a year of celibacy. But about a month into my freshman year, I met a girl at a party."

I stopped and took a sip of water from the glass Alice had placed in front of me.

"Her name was Theresa, and I thought she was gorgeous, in the way girls appeared in magazines, fake. I've come to detest that look and don't have anything to do with women who appear as mannequins." I really didn't want to talk about this. I could feel my heart rate going up just thinking about that night.

"She came on to me all night, and being the best-looking girl at the party, I received envious looks from the other lads. My roommate kept nudging me and encouraging me to talk to her. I finally summoned up enough courage to walk over to her and introduce myself. Instead of shaking my offered hand, she grabbed my junk and raised her eyes to mine in an invitation."

I could feel the sweat breaking out on my forehead. I swiped with the back of my hand and took another swig of water.

"Then she led me off to a vacant bedroom upstairs. She locked the door and pushed me onto the bed. I was so turned on, I just did as she told me to do. Then she proceeded to do a striptease down to her bra and G-string."

I stopped to collect my thoughts, resting my head in my hands for a moment and rubbing my eyes.

"Laughlin, have you ever told anyone this story before?" I shook my head no. " It won't be as bad as you think. In fact, I think you will feel as if a burden has been lifted when you are done. Please take your time, as there is no need to rush. I am a safe place, and you know I have tremendous respect for you. It's okay to share and discuss this like adults."

I straightened up and drained my water glass. "Then, Theresa ground her way over to me and undid my zipper. Something in me snapped. Every fantasy I'd ever had was coming to life, and I was suddenly desperate for release. I grabbed Theresa and threw her on the bed. Her coaxing smile egging me on, I ripped her G-string off and ripped open her bra. She licked her lips and told me to hurry. I took my shoelaces and tied her to the bed. I poked and prodded and licked and sucked until I couldn't take anymore, and then I took her. I came quite quickly, but I don't remember if she did. I untied her, and we both lay back on the bed. After a few minutes, she grabbed my junk and began to pump me. She asked me to take her anally. I was so excited, I was hard as a rock the instant the words left her mouth."

I paused a moment before continuing. "She moved onto her hands and knees in front of me and gyrated towards my cock. I lubed her up and took her anally. I started slow, as I had never had intercourse before, and I was told that anal should be slower and gentler."

I paused again, steeling myself for the second half of the story.

"Theresa was not interested in gentle. As soon as I slid

partway in, she shoved her backside over my cock. Clearly, the woman was well experienced, and I didn't want to disappoint. She played with herself while I pummeled her ass, and when I spent, we both collapsed on the bed in a flurry of panting breath and sweaty limbs."

Alice poured more water, and I guzzled it down. "She had not said a word to me and, a few minutes later, got up and dressed and threw me a wink on her way out the door. I thought I'd hit the jackpot. I lay there for a bit, digesting all the sex I'd just had and analyzing my performance. I thought I had done pretty well for a virgin."

I sat back and let out a deep sigh. "I never saw Theresa again, but she managed to haunt me all through the next three years. She started a rumor that I was a savage animal and had attacked her, dragging her upstairs, tying her to a bed, and assaulting her."

Funny, thinking back, no one else at the party negated her story, everyone conveniently forgetting she came on to me. "The legend of my sexual escapade grew, and by the time I graduated, I'd not had a single date. It seemed every female I introduced myself to was terrified of me. She had knackered me good. Even had I wanted to do anything with anyone, I couldn't. On top of all of that, I felt terrible. I felt guilt, and worse, I felt like a creep. I didn't know what had been expected of me. I swam in deep water with no restraint, and I paid for it."

Alice sat back, her facial expression blank. "What did you do after school, for sex? You mentioned you didn't date."

"Once I graduated, I released my pent-up sexual tension with a service. It took a while, but eventually, I found a few women who knew what I liked, and I had them exclusively for a few years."

I took another sip of water and sat back for a moment,

noting Alice's earlier statement had been correct. There was a sort of relief I felt in sharing that story.

"It sounds like you have found ways to work with your issue. Why seek me out now?"

"Fast forward to the last six weeks. I have been in a relationship, a live-in relationship with an amazing woman." I spent the next twenty minutes telling Alice about Suri.

"The sex thing isn't the problem, as Suri and I like the same things. In every way, she is perfect for me. Before coming to Scotland, I told her I didn't know what I could offer beyond a fun time. I'm damaged goods. Why would anyone want to have anything long-term with me? I am not a good man, you can clearly tell from my story. Alice, you can tell that I am beastly. I just can't get past my feelings of inadequacy as a man, a potential mate. Suri is… well, she is special, and I feel she deserves the best possible person for her. Am I really it?"

"I believe your issues have nothing to do with your current situation. It runs much deeper than your problem committing to Suri. Your inadequacy stems from your childhood. The college crisis magnified something else from your past, and you were pushed to a nasty foregone conclusion. Go back to your childhood, Laughlin, and allow yourself to go back to the first time doubt settled in your heart, sometime between the age of four and six. Learn to let go of what you find. Allow yourself to let go of those things, so you may have a future with your woman."

I considered Alice's words on my way home. There was only one person I knew who might be able to help me uncover events from such a tender age—Henry Fitzwilliam, my parents' dearest friend.

Chapter 13

Suri

Laughlin seemed different since his meeting in the city, more introspective and his expression not as shuttered. I could tell he was wrestling with something and wished I could help. But something told me it was his past, of which I was still hugely uninformed.

It didn't matter to me that I didn't know a lot about Laughlin's previous personal life. I wasn't dating the old him, but the person I woke up to each morning. That man fulfilled me in so many ways. He spoiled me rotten with his time, the mind-blowing sex and, of course, the gifts he insisted on giving me.

I needed the alone time I got while he worked, spending my time reading and writing, in his enormous library or outside by the lagoon and, of course, swimming and doing yoga. I kept in touch with Shelley every day, which also took up some time, and she kept asking me if there were any more of his at home.

So far, my time in Scotland had been incredibly self-indulgent, and though I knew things wouldn't stay that way forever, I almost felt guilty to have so much time on my hands. Although even that was about to change, as we had guests arriving from Canada.

We left for the airport in two vehicles. Thor, Laughlin's head of security, took the rhino GX, which had room for seven passengers. We took the slightly less ostentatious GMC Nightfall, which held five passengers in addition to me.

I took advantage of the silence to chant for a safe, fun, and productive time—my first chance to spend time with Laughlin's fishing friends. Of course, I knew who they really were, but I also knew they enjoyed fishing, and Laughlin had reserved us ferry passage for the next day to take us to the Outer Hebrides, where he had several small beach cottages and a fishing liner booked.

The group was coming through the one security station the hangar provided. As I gazed from face to face, I was surprised, as these people seemed like friends and family, not a team of fishing buddies.

In the lead, was a handsome gentleman who was probably just hitting his late fifties. He walked and interacted with a vigor that belied his age. Right behind him, was a younger version of him, but more Greek god meets movie star. His energy was vibrant but seemed to house a gentle spirit. His arm was wrapped around a woman who took my breath away.

It wasn't her beauty, although she had it in spades. She was young, maybe early twenties, but with the oldest eyes I'd ever seen. Whoever she was, there was a wisdom that went far beyond her age, the oldest young person I'd ever seen.

She was busy chatting with the man behind her, who looked like an army veteran. He was older than she by a few years and, like her, had prematurely aged eyes. I wondered if they were related and perhaps had seen some horrible atrocity that had given them both ancient-looking eyes.

Along with him, were five others who all bore a similar look—deadly. Then at the end of the line, was a huge Scotsman. Beside me, I felt Laughlin chuckle.

"Do you know that big one at the end of the line?" I whispered. I didn't want my voice to carry and appear rude.

"Oh, aye, I do. He is Declan Campbell, a millionaire turned security guard, an old friend, and a newly made member of the Order."

I wanted to ask how that happened, but everyone was through the line and making their way to us with huge smiles on their faces.

Laughlin embraced the first man, the eldest in the group. "Geoff, it's good to see you." They pounded on each other for a moment. Then Geoff pulled away, and his eyes traveled to mine. We held each other's gaze for a moment, and I saw that this man, Geoff, was calculating me. His eyes had a deep intelligence, but his scrutiny did not make me uncomfortable in the least.

"I am Suri," I said, holding out my hand. When our grips entwined, I felt a bolt of energy shoot down my arm and flare into our grasp. I knew he felt it because his eyes rounded for the briefest of seconds before settling back to his friendly, calculating one.

"It is a pleasure to meet you, Suri. Let me introduce you to my family. This is my son and heir apparent, Adam, and his wife, Montana."

Adam's eyes held curiosity when he looked at me. I could feel him digging and had the oddest feeling that the man could see my soul. He had the discernment and intelligence of his father, put in a different wrapping. Before I could think more about this, Montana and I squeezed hands. And I had what I call a psychic slap.

I saw her in a hospital bed. Her husband, Adam, was with another man who looked exactly like her, a twin? I looked up at the giant, who in turn was watching Adam's wife intensely. He was her personal guard. I knew it. She smiled at me, and I saw a beautiful soul; more than that, I saw a soul that had passed and come back.

"Montana, I am so happy to meet you. It will be nice to have a female amongst all this male testosterone."

She grinned, her eyes lighting up. "I think we shall have a wonderful time getting to know each other." She winked, so only I could see. It was hard not to laugh at her antics, and I'd bet she kept all these men on their toes.

"I take it you don't fish?"

"Not a chance. We will have to find other things to divert our attention." She turned then and embraced Laughlin, and the three of them moved towards Thor, whom they also embraced like old friends. It was a friendly group.

Next, I met Eddy, his team, Luke, Steve, Rob, Mike, and J2. Then came the giant. He and Laughlin were of similar height and build. But where Laughlin was chiseled and had dark hair and eyes, this guy had a mess of red curls that came down to his shoulders, and his eyes were not one color. They seemed to shift in the light, so it was hard to tell the actual color.

"Well, if it isn't the brawny Scot; about time you came back to Scotland." Laughlin embraced the giant with no back-slapping, like the others, but an intense squeeze. This man was someone he trusted. "Declan, this is my girl, Suri."

Declan regarded me, almost as intensely as Geoff had. I did my best to be open to the scrutiny, and as the seconds passed, a slow smile finally began to emerge on the giant's face. "Laughlin, I don't know how ye got this lass, but you are a lucky bastard."

I let out a stream of tinkling laughter while Declan let out a deep, guffawing laugh. Laughlin shook his head and muttered about it being a long week while the giant and I continued to laugh.

He was such an open, honest man. I was surprised he wasn't with a woman. He had a story, they all did, and I couldn't wait to learn more about them. For the first time since learning we had guests, I felt excitement.

Chapter 14

Laughlin

After six hours of travel, we were finally safely tucked away in a two-hundred-year-old stone cottage on the edge of Benbecula, in South Uist. Our welcoming party consisted of a fully stocked bar fridge with all of Suri's favorite wines and a refrigerator with all of Suri's favorite foods.

"How did you manage this? You must have sent a list ahead." She did a slow strut from the kitchen to where I was standing, wrapping her arms around my waist and squeezing my ass. She reached up and drew my face towards her, sliding her tongue in my mouth. She roamed my mouth with her tongue while her hands kneaded my ass.

"Mmm, is this my reward for being so organized? If so, I must remember to do this on all of our trips together."

Without realizing it, I spoke of the future and one where she and I were together. If she noticed, she said nothing but continued exploring me and giving me a massive hard-on.

Finally, she pulled away and grabbed my stiff shaft through my shorts.

"I'll be back for you later," she promised, releasing my John Thomas. She grabbed a bottle of wine, and we headed out to our private beach to meet with the others. I had set up five cottages, though I only owned two. I was friends with the others' owner and had taken over the lot of them for a week.

We were the first to arrive outside. "Laughlin, this is stunning," she commented. " I can't wait to get to know everyone better and go swimming. I heard this part of the ocean has a warm current that pulls in a variety of sea life."

Naturally, she didn't refer to only people when she said *everyone*, but animals too. I had noticed that when she was in the water, the sea life seemed to be drawn to her. I had personally witnessed more dolphins, seals, and turtles when she was in the water than I had ever before.

Here in Southern Uist, there was a warm southern current that made this area tropical. The water swarmed with whales, dolphins, sharks, seals, and much more. She would have to tread carefully. Unlike Turkey and Greece, the sea was more treacherous.

"Suri, do me this one favor… please be careful; this is very different from any sea you have been in. It is deceiving. Tropical and lovely where the two seas meet but very treacherous farther out. With us out fishing, you and Montana will no doubt want to explore. Thor has two men keeping watch on our gathering. But that won't help if you're too far out and a current grabs you."

She studied me for a moment, "Be careful, my gruff Scots man, you sound like you are worried." Her teasing response did nothing to alleviate a sense of misgiving starting to build. Maybe bringing her here was a mistake.

"I promise, Laughlin, I will be careful and do my utmost to behave. You don't have to regret your decision about bringing me here." She gazed at me thoughtfully, her eyes looking unfocused yet penetrating.

"Geez, woman, are you a mind reader now? I'll have to stop thinking, or you may find out my deepest thoughts." She laughed and turned her gaze down the beach. The others were making their way over, and it was time to get drinks and food.

When I hired the locals to set up the cottages for me, I made sure the bars and coolers were well stocked with beer, which most of the men preferred. I also made sure we had a selection of food for tonight's beach clambake along with various appetizers.

Suri and I set up the Adirondack chairs in a circle around the large fire pit.

"This reminds me of the Caymans," Adam said, arriving first.

"Oh, I loved the Caymans. We had so much fun there," Montana responded.

"Yeah," Adam added as he sat, "if you forget the dolphins and the gunfire, it was perfect."

My ears perked up at dolphins. God help us, not another ocean lover. Montana's eyes found Suri's.

"I'll tell you tomorrow, without these guys. It's a long story," she said, indicating the rest, who were now grabbing their chairs. "We'll have a lot of time to talk."

"That doesn't sound good," Declan said, dropping down on Montana's other side. "This lass is a handful. Well, not for me, aye, but for this lot." He roared out his laughter, and Adam and the others added in their laughter. They had a private joke going on that I was oblivious to.

My eyes sought Geoff, who had been watching the exchange with his usual intensity.

He smiled at me. "Don't worry, Laughlin, you'll soon see, we have more in common than you realize." Ominous words repeated in my mind as the night carried on, and copious amounts of alcohol were consumed.

It wasn't long after that when Adam put music on his iPad, and the lasses were on their feet, dancing in the firelight. There couldn't have been two more different looking women. Montana and Suri were almost identical in height. But Suri was muscular and curvy and every man's wet dream.

Montana was lithe and muscular. Her only roundness was in her breasts and ass. Every other part of her showed a warrior's body. Glancing to the men around the fire, they all held gazes of appreciation for Montana, except Adam's eyes, which had so much love that I was almost uncomfortable.

Declan's gaze was unreadable, shuttered. He was protecting himself, and I realized he was in love with Montana —poor bastard. As my eyes bounced back to the ladies, they were having so much fun. I smiled, seeing Suri so light-hearted. She moved like a dancer, her beautiful body moving in delicious patterns. I felt my cock harden in my shorts. Damn, the woman was magical.

"She is quite something, your Suri. You will have to share with us the story of how you two met."

I nodded, lost in the dancing flames and the two undulating women who seemed ensnared by them. "Aye, there is much to tell. As we have an early morning, we should find our beds."

I pulled my gaze from the hypnotic flames to Geoff's face. His grin spoke loudly of what he saw, my turmoil as evident to him as it had been to Alice. I hadn't had time to meet and question Sir Henry regarding my childhood, and until I did, I wasn't prepared to spill on my commitment issues. This was Templar's business, and I would stay on topic.

"Wise," Geoff answered. Standing, he gained everyone's attention and said it was time to wrap things up as the morning would come fast. We said our goodnights and parted ways. I followed Suri into the house, with only the moonlight coming through the windows to light her path. But she was easy to see in the darkness, as the fire flames still danced on her skin.

She stopped in a pool of moonlight and lifted her head towards me. Her eyes glistened in the white light, a new light provided by the moon. She curled her finger at me, and as she did so, she dropped to her knees.

"I would love to suck your cock, Sir." A smile lifted the corners of her mouth. Her words and position of submission on the floor were enough to have me straining in my shorts. But her eyes said so much more. An entire universe danced in there and had me wondering where she was and what she was thinking.

"It's late, and I think maybe we should go to bed." I gave her the out because we'd both had a lot to drink.

"Please, I need to feel you in my mouth. I need you to take me in that way."

That was all I needed. Who was I to deny this beautiful woman anything? I moved directly in front of her and dropped my shorts. She kept her head level with my cock, but her eyes were on mine as she took me in her mouth. Her tongue went to work immediately, and I found it challenging to maintain her gaze.

When she moaned, it reverberated all along my length. I reached for her head and grasped her hair tightly as she liked. She placed her hands on my thighs to stabilize herself. She closed her eyes then and softened her throat, taking my length deeper than she ever had before.

I held her head still while we both acclimatized to the new sensation. I began to take her mouth and throat with slow strokes. Suri was one continual moan, unleashing all kinds of feelings in me. When I could take no more, I increased my pumps' speed and, within seconds, released my seed deep in her throat. She was still moaning, setting off a chain reaction that affected my orgasm. It was the longest release I could remember ever having.

When I released her hair, I helped her stand, scooped her, and carried her to bed. "Suri, that was magical, thank you."

Her eyes were already closed, and she was asleep by the time I laid her down. I busied myself in the bathroom and then set a bottle of water and two acetaminophens on her nightstand.

I jumped in bed and cuddled up behind her, tugging her backside into my groin.

"I love you," she said and fell back to sleep.

I froze. Had she just used the L-word? I was so screwed. What if I couldn't love her back? What if all I was capable of was what we already had?

I got out of bed and texted Henry Fitzwilliam: *If six am isn't too early, I need to talk.*

Henry: *I'm awake. What can I do for you, for mo leanbh?*

He used the term of endearment for my child. He was the only one I could remember who ever had. I felt tears sting my eyes. What the hell was wrong with me?

Me: *What did I witness when I was four that I cannot remember?*

My phone beeped, and Henry's name had popped up on the screen. I answered it, walking into the other room. "Henry."

"Laughlin, what has your knickers in such a tight knot that you're asking me about your childhood at one am?"

"It's a long story, Henry, but I'll shorten it for the late hour. You remember what happened to me in my freshman year in college?"

"I do; what of it?"

"I decided to seek out counseling. I have a woman in my life, and if I can keep my shit together and embrace the gift God has seen fit to bless me with, then I may end up marrying her. But my counselor said what I'm suffering from happened long before my college days. She said around age four, no older than six. So, I ask ye, what the hell happened to me?"

I could hear Henry uncork one of his crystal decanters and then the splashing of fine whiskey being poured into a crystal decanter.

"I advised your father long ago to tell you the truth. Perhaps his premature death kept him from doing so."

He paused, and while I waited, the knot in my gut grew tighter, making breathing difficult.

"Your mother died in childbirth, Laughlin, and you witnessed her death."

It felt as though the blood froze in my veins as I digested this. A memory slammed into my conscious mind with a velocity that made me physically fall into a chair.

The maid, Annie, had screamed and woken me up. "What's wrong with mother?" I was standing at the threshold of her bedroom with my hands over my ears, having been woken up by the racket. Just then, Annie moved to my side and took my hand. As she led me away, my father said, "Forget what you have seen, Laughlin. Forget this night in its entirety."

"What happened to the baby?"

"Dead, it didn't last the night."

"I see, and I thank you, Henry, for telling me the truth."

"Laughlin, listen to me. Your father was a brilliant, capable man and my best friend through life. He was not a warm, loving presence, and with your mother's death, I'm afraid you felt abandoned by love. Maybe your shrink friend is right, and it all began when you lost your mother who loved you ferociously."

I was silent, sifting through the onslaught of emotions that were plowing through me.

"Don't let her death define you, Laughlin. If you have a lass, open yourself to her. Allow her in. If she is the right one, as you suspect, then things will turn out for the best."

"I don't know what any of us men of the Order are doing with women in our lives, Henry. We are putting them at risk."

"I know it seems that way, but, Laughlin, there is also much life to live, to enjoy. Is it not better to have truly lived than to have never lived at all?"

I had no response to that. Wasn't that the crux of it all, that very issue? I knew how to live alone. I had learned how to run a great life independently. What I didn't know was how to really live. I had been in the shadow for a long time, and maybe now was the time to step out into the light.

"Thank you, Henry. I have a lot to think about."

"Bring your lass over to dinner sometime; let me meet her."

"Aye, I will, good night."

I hung up the phone and crawled back into the bed and Suri's warmth. She was real, and she was here, and maybe that could be enough. Only time would tell.

Chapter 15

Suri

Montana and I were lying out on beach loungers enjoying the beautiful day. Even in summer, hot days in Scotland were rare, and today was perfect with not a cloud in the sky. "So how did you meet Adam?" I asked, dying to get to know this woman better.

She shaded her eyes as she turned her head in my direction. "Teen crush. He went to art school with my brother."

"I knew it. My Spidey senses told me that about Adam as I observed him in the customs line."

Montana laughed. "Yeah, he has that vibe."

"You have a unique vibe too, Montana, and the oldest eyes I have ever seen. Have you had a tough life?"

She did not answer at first, then she quietly said, "Define *tough*."

I liked this woman. She was so different than anyone I'd ever met before, but she did have a trait that reminded me of myself and my bestie, Shelley. She was a survivor. "Fair question, and to answer, I define tough as being exceptional or unusual circumstances that form a person to be more than they ever could or wanted to be."

She shaded her eyes as she regarded me. "I like that definition, and I totally agree. Okay, so in a nutshell, when I was young, my mother died. We, meaning my brothers and I, should have been raised by my father. He worked on the oil rigs on the other side of Canada, and we only saw him twice a year."

"How many brothers do you have?"

"Three, including my twin. My eldest brother had the honor of raising my perfect brothers and me." She laughed at her words, and I joined in. Even though I didn't know the circumstances, I could see her being a handful.

"My middle brother is an artist and my husband's best friend. My eldest works for Geoff, and my youngest, my twin, runs our record company."

"So, he is a musician?"

She smirked. "Where have you been living, Suri, Siberia? You seriously don't know who I am?"

My blank expression set off peals of laughter, and I found myself amused by her easy demeanor.

"Have you heard of the rock band, Behind Blue Eyes?"

I shook my head in the negative. "I'm out of every loop about everything but yoga. I have worked basically fourteen hours a day after college and then married a man who basically enslaved me and then tried to kill me. I have been free of him for just over a year now. So, I guess you could say that I've been living in Siberia. A frozen wasteland, just not in Russia."

Any traces of amusement fell away from her. "Well, fuck me, that is brutal and deserves a drink." Montana went inside, came back with two full glasses of white wine and handed me one. "Cheers, Suri, to women of great strength."

"Cheers," I said and clicked my wine glass to hers. "You

know it's your turn again, and you left off with telling me of your brothers."

Montana took a swig of wine, adding, "Mm, I love wine, and this is exquisite. You have good taste. Adam says I drink too much of it, but I say, I don't do drugs, and I don't generally drink anything but wine, and I don't smoke, so suck it up, buttercup."

I was just taking a sip of wine myself and instantly choked on it as her words made me laugh. "Oh my god," I said when I finally calmed down, "who are you, and where have you been all my life?"

"Aye, in Canada, eh?" She did a perfect imitation of Declan's thick brogue that set off a convulsion fit of coughing and laugher.

"Montana, you're killing me," I wheezed after I'd finally calmed down.

"Well, it's nice to clown around. I only do so when I feel comfortable. Eddy is my best friend from childhood. The guy bailed me out so many times, but when we just hang out together, we laugh a lot."

"I'm glad you're comfortable around me. I feel the same way around you, and I'm delighted we met."

She shaded her eyes from the sun as she said, "Me too, mo caraid."

"What does mo caraid mean?"

"My friend."

I smiled, and although the two words spoken in English were simple, they sounded heartfelt in Scottish. Montana was a woman I could trust, and I opened up to her, telling her about Edward and the yoga retreat and how I met Laughlin in Turkey. I didn't leave anything out. When I was done with my story, the wine bottle was also finished.

Montana left and came back with two bottles of water.

"Here," she said, handing me one. "If Adam asks, yes, I drank water."

I downed it, not realizing how dehydrated I was. "Thank you. I needed that."

"Me too, and you know what else I need? A swim. The last one in is a rotten egg." Montana took off, her long, athletic legs carrying her into the surf seconds before me. We swam out, about a hundred feet from shore, and tread in the buoyant water.

"This is so different than any water I've swum in. I've been to Scotland before but not the Hebrides. Did you know I own a castle?" Montana looked at me smugly. Her facial expression was so direct, it was hard to imagine her being deceptive.

"I think we established the fact that I don't, or didn't, know a thing about you until today."

"Pooh! You make it so hard to be smug when you are so sincerely open. I truly like you, Suri."

We bobbed in the water, the sun glistening and making the tips of the gentle waves look like sparkling jewels.

"The ocean is my favorite place," she said so quietly that I almost didn't hear her. Then she added, "It is special to me."

"Me too," I answered. "I want to show you something. Let's swim back until we can touch bottom."

Gazing around, Montana said, "I have a better idea. Let's swim out to that sandbank."

I looked to the spot she pointed out and back to the shore, trying to gauge the return trip's distance. Going out much farther would take us dangerously close to the treacherous waters Laughlin had warned me about. But I was feeling emboldened by the wind and conceded. As we made our way to the sandy bank, I felt the shift in the current we moved through and hoped it didn't pick up intensity. As soon as we landed, I sat at the edge of the bank, looking out to the endless sea. I began to chant, and while I chanted, I held out my hands, opening up my energy to the environment and hoping there were dolphins near enough to feel me.

We didn't have long to wait. Five heads popped up, and Montana squealed with delight. She didn't wait a beat before diving back in and swimming out to them. I followed, with a deepening sense of dread. I felt we were too far from land and was fearful of the strong current and the distance we had to swim.

Thankfully, the dolphin's interest in us was equal to ours in them, and they swam closer to us. Montana was touching them with zero fear. I could tell she was not a novice like I was. I tentatively reached out a hand to touch the one closest to me. The smooth rubbery skin felt different than I expected.

They chittered at us, and Montana, being a vocalist, could imitate the sounds they were making as she chittered in response. They seemed as intrigued by us as we were by them —a sense of wonder, a sacredness at the moment, that allowed me to feel connected to the sea. Tears formed at the corners of my eyes as I stroked the beautiful animals.

It was a rare, entirely in the moment experience—the water's temperature, the sounds both far and near, the sun glistening all hit me in a wave of consciousness. At that moment, I was just a human being feeling and noticing things.

I was not Suri, the person, but Suri the being, and Montana seemed to be just as in the moment as I was, appearing more mermaid than human. Her energy was vibrating, adding depth to her already intriguing character.

Then a thought slammed into my consciousness, breaking the magic of the moment. I gazed back and saw that our little island was no more. It was time to go back. "We should start swimming back, Montana. The sand bar is underwater."

She chittered goodbye to the animals, both of us giving them some last-minute rubs, and then we began our return swim.

"At least the water is coming in and taking us with it," I huffed. I wasn't out of shape, but this was a lot harder than swimming in Laughlin's pool.

Montana, who had been ahead of me, turned towards me. "Hey, do you think that's the guys?" I looked at where she was pointing and watched the boat that was making its way towards us. As it sped closer, I could tell it wasn't the fishing boat Laughlin had rented. It looked more like one of those racing boats, and I wondered what it was doing way over here.

"That's not the guys; hurry, swim as fast as you can for shore. Whoever they are, they are coming in too fast, and they may be part of a group that has made a few attempts on my life."

We picked up our pace and managed to get to the shore with the boat about fifty feet behind us. We were exhausted, but we stumbled out of the sea and ran for the cottage. The boat was pulling up, and men were yelling and giving chase. I prayed Thor's men were aware of what was going on.

"What the hell?" Montana finally got out when we made it inside the cottage and locked the doors behind us. "If they want us, this isn't going to stop them, Suri."

Laughlin had given me a walkie-talkie. Where the hell did I put it?

"Let's go into the bathroom. There is a window that opens to the back. With any luck, whoever they are will be focused on breaking in the front."

We raced to the bedroom as the front door slammed open. I grabbed the walkie off the bed, and we ran into the bathroom, locking the door. "Help, mayday, whatever, there are assailants on land, SOS."

Beside me, Montana was quietly laughing as she tried to catch her breath. "What is so funny?" I hissed.

"You. Could you be any more cliché?" Then she stood and

took the curtain rod down and peeked out the back window. "Okay, get out there; I'll hold them off."

"With a shower rod? Are you crazy?"

"A little, but I am also deadly. Trust me, if anyone gets through the door before I'm out the window, they will regret it." With a shake of my head, I pulled myself up through the narrow opening, glancing both ways before I dropped down. I started running when I heard Montana drop to the earth and follow me.

"Where are you going?" she huffed as she caught up to me.

"See that tree coverage. That is where the guards are hiding."

"What makes you think they are still there?" she asked, keeping pace with me. Before I could answer, I heard yelling, and gunshots rang out. Both of us instinctively ducked down, but no bullets came our way. Our security must have gotten to the cottage and were engaged in gunfire.

When we hit the tree coverage and found a hiding spot, we threw ourselves behind a fallen tree. "Laughlin, can you hear me? We are under attack. Come in."

"At least you didn't sound like some cheesy movie that time," Montana commented as she struggled to catch her breath.

I leaned back, trying to slow my racing heart. Nearby, a snap cracked somewhere close by that made both of us freeze. Montana was on her haunches gazing around. She reached for a branch that was a good two inches thick and motioned me to follow her.

Of the two of us, she was far more prepared. The idea of how she came by her skill set made a shiver go down my spine. I realized now that she never finished her *hard-knock story*, and instead, I'd spilled the beans on my sordid past.

I heard a scuffle then a thwack and then the sound of a

body hitting the ground. Montana ducked back, holding a gun and handing me the stick. "I'm going to assume you don't know how to use it?"

I shook my head and wondered, not for the first time, who the hell she was. I followed her back to the edge of the woods. We couldn't see anything up ahead by the cottage, and I wondered what happened to all the men who had jumped off the boat. We crept along the edge of the foliage. All the while, Montana held the gun cocked and ready to be fired if need be.

"Montana, squat agus rolla!" was shouted, and before I could process the owner of the voice or decipher the words, I was on the ground, Montana beside me. Gunfire rang out, and something behind us thudded to the ground.

Then Declan emerged from the woods looking like a Highlander, his red curls glistening with sweat or water—I wasn't sure which—and naked, except for his kilt, which I presumed he'd worn fishing.

"A bheil thu ceart gu leòr mo ghaol," he said to Montana while helping her to her feet.

"I'm fine, you giant ox. Where is everyone else?"

Laughlin came peeling around the cottage's corner before Declan could answer and, spotting us, came running over, Adam and Eddy right on his heels.

I was so relieved that a sob rose in my throat as Laughlin pulled me to him. "Suri, are you okay? What happened?"

"I'll tell you what happened," Declan interrupted. "Someone leaked our location and came after the lasses while we were gone. That's what bloody happened."

"I'll have the team put this body with the others, and then we figure this out," Eddy said after examining the clearing."

"There's another body in the brush back there. I knocked him out and took his gun." Montana spoke with not even a quiver in her voice. I think she was the strongest woman I'd ever met.

"Already tied up; at least he is alive and we can question him," Declan added.

I couldn't stop shaking, but that was probably due to the extended swim and lack of food, along with the shock. Without Laughlin all but carrying me, I wouldn't have made it back on my own.

Thankfully, there were no bodies to be seen, already having been removed. Laughlin walked me into our bathroom. Seeing the rod gone and the window, still open brought back our narrow escape, and I broke down.

Laughlin stood in the shower, holding me tight, not the slightest bit concerned that the floor was getting soaked.

"Shh, you're okay now, Suri. Nothing can get you while I'm here."

I gripped him tightly until my heartbeat slowed down and I could finally breathe. We exited half an hour later, to find food and beverages set up like last evening. A somber group assembled at the fire as the sun was setting.

"So, which one of you would like to start?"

Chapter 16

Laughlin

I glanced around the fire, at the six of us, while the rest were dealing with the bodies and questioning the lone survivor. Geoff and Declan wore grim expressions as Montana told of spotting the boat and the brisk swim to shore and into hiding.

I watched Suri; she was easy to read. I knew that Montana left out specific points by Suri's facial responses to Montana's words. As the tale unfolded, Adam's expression was very different from his father's or Declan's. He saw something else.

"How far out were you?" he interrupted Montana. The first crack in her veneer showed for just a moment before she shuttered her expression back to a bland earnestness. Instead of answering, her gaze went to Suri.

"Not far, Adam, about seventy-five feet." The right answer, as that was well within the boundary I had set, but she was lying, and I knew it. Adam had a gaze that stripped one's soul for all to see. I had never seen a look quite like that before. He would be a fantastic leader for the Templars when Geoff passed on the torch.

Suri blushed at his scrutiny but held his eye. I wanted to protect her, to punch Adam in the face and tell him to back off. But Suri had chosen to answer the question directed to another, and I would allow it to play out, for now.

As Adam continued to stare Suri down, her defenses broke. "It is all my fault." Tears welled in her beautiful eyes. "I heard you mention dolphins at the fire last night, and well, they are here. Well, I thought they may be close and took her to see them. It was on our way back to shore that we saw the boat coming to shore at a fairly fast pace." She wiped a single tear from her cheek. "We could have gotten to shore faster, although I don't know if that would have changed anything. I would have taken the same actions, only we may have gotten further away."

"Aye, good point, lass," Declan broke in. "The real issue here is who they are and what they want."

"I think I can answer that." Eddy materialized out of the gloom and into the light cast by the fire.

"What have you learned?" Geoff asked.

"The leader of the band got away, and his second lieutenant was killed. This guy has been purposely uninformed. But we did learn he is a member of SOG." Damn, if SOG was in Scotland, the entire chapter may be at risk.

"There is one more thing," Eddy added, looking at me. "The leader of this coup's name is Alastair Sinclair, a Scots. Do you know him?" Eddy looked from me to Declan, but we both shook our heads in the negative.

"Just because he has a Scottish name doesn't mean he lives in Scotland. He could be from the middle east, the U.S., or even Canada."

"Aye, it's true," Declan added, "but if he's a Sinclair by

birth, then he may be working for the church, and who was the target, Suri or Montana?"

"I don't think the question is as easy as that, Declan. I'm sure you and Geoff heard of my father's death. I believe it was murder and not an accident. I was in Turkey to do reconnaissance on his death, and Suri ran into me after witnessing a crime aimed at the Masons."

The group remained silent.

"I don't think it was a coincidence, and Suri is also a Sinclair. Somehow she is related to this mystery, but I'm not sure how as yet."

Declan and Geoff exchanged a look that told me they had another theory. Geoff had mentioned earlier minor accidents occurring with senior members of Mason chapters all across Canada.

"Maybe today was purely coincidental," Geoff spoke. "Montana could be a target for me, Adam, or even Declan. His friend Charles Muir was on Templar business in Cambridge, England and went missing just last week."

I didn't know Charles well, but I had been introduced to him by Declan several years back. He was a teacher and scholar, specializing in Scottish history. "There must be a breakdown in communication within the Order, and someone has access to classified information. How else would they find out we came here?"

"I think you have a personal breach in your household maybe. We can discuss that in due time. I brought Adam and Montana here for a reason. As you already know, Laughlin, Adam is my only son and although I have ill prepared him for his role in the Order, what gets shared among us, he must be a part of."

Whatever Geoff was going to share, Adam's face remained impassive as if he knew what was coming. "Several years back,

I doctored some records in the Edinburgh library, historical records of my son's ancestry and Montana's."

Both Adam and Montana's faces showed some surprise, but not Declan's. Somehow he had found out.

"Geoff told me when I confronted him about the missing information in the archives. I still have deep connections to information, having owned the Flying Scotsman," Declan confessed. "It wasn't until I found an old parish birth record book that I knew something was missing."

I was growing frustrated. Three times, Suri had been a target. Whatever was happening in the Canadian chapter, on Geoff's end, must be singular. I knew Suri was the target but still didn't know why. "Gentlemen, while I find this all fascinating, I hardly see the connection between this and my father or Suri."

Geoff's eyes gleamed in the firelight. "It could be nothing directly," he finally conceded. "What I'm trying to say is someone is going to a lot of trouble to remove anyone who has connections to the original Templars."

"I agree. Maybe if you tell me what you changed in the history books, what you're trying to hide. Be plain if need be, Geoff, but tell me what is so important."

"We have an imposter deep in the Order, and they know about Suri's family and the connection to the treasure. They know that approximately five hundred years ago, a young lass left Scotland with only the cloak on her back. That same lass married a man who became the most powerful leader of his time and began a line of warrior children to help keep the Templars' secrets."

The fire chose that moment to pop and hiss, making all of us jump. "What of Suri and the treasure?" Beside me, I felt the tension rolling off of Suri in waves.

When Geoff answered, he was looking at Suri, not me.

"Your family, the Sinclairs, left Scotland one hundred and fifty years ago, Suri. Your father isn't John Stamos. That is a cover name. He is Cecil de Sinclair, our eastern Grand Master and a descendant of Mary Campbell, the same girl who left Scotland five hundred years ago, the same woman whose half-sister created Declan's line and Montana's family."

I was reeling with Geoff's reveal, and I wasn't the only one. It seemed all but Declan was in shock at this news.

"Ancestrally speaking, Declan and Montana's great-grandmas ten times removed were half-sisters." The night seemed to deepen, closing us in the circle of light. Inside me, a door opened and closed. There was way more to this conspiracy than I could have imagined.

Declan's face remained stoically informed while Adam, Montana, and Suri were like fish gasping for air, their mouths moving with unasked questions. Despite being out in the open, I felt as if walls were closing in, creating suffocation I could barely tolerate. My only problem was what did these three branches have to do with the treasure, and why now?

"Suri married the heir apparent as Cecil never had a son. But what Cecil didn't know is that Edward Stanhope Sr. is the North American head of SOG. That organization has become desperate for information now that the eastern seaboard has been under intense scrutiny regarding the fall and subsequent death of Edward, Cecil's inheritor to the Templar throne."

Beside me, Suri stiffened at this information. She'd had no idea and dredging up her history after a trying day was too much, even for this strong woman. Across from me, I could see Montana had shut down and was lost in thought, Adam's hand her only anchor to the here and now. Giving Adam a look he interpreted correctly, he stood.

"That is a lot to process, Dad. We should get some sleep and perhaps take this to a more secure location. I say we pack up in the morning and go back to Roswell to come up with a plan."

I stood as well and pulled Suri to her feet. "I agree. Thank you, gentlemen. We will see you at first light."

Chapter 17

Suri

Nothing was as it seemed, was the repeating mantra in my head on the trip back to the mainland. The weather was wet and stormy, almost as if the environment was born of the group's low disposition.

After we arrived back, the sun came out. The storm, already making its way through the mainland, had left sweet-smelling foliage in its wake. After setting up the security detail, the men closeted themselves in Laughlin's work office. This was a completely different room than what he referred to as his day office. The work office looked like a CIA bunker, at least the way I imagined one would look.

Leaving Montana and me time to pick up where we left off, we took snacks and drinks to the pool. As both of us were water people, there was no better place than Laughlin's lagoon. We were lying out on the floating mats when she asked me what I thought about the conversation from the past evening. My only response was to shrug. I wasn't thinking about it, the fringes of thoughts on the matter scary enough for me to push aside for now.

"Montana, did you learn anything more about your back story?"

"No, but I will. Declan will tell me now that the cat is out of the bag. How are you taking it? Come on; spill already."

I sighed as I closed my eyes against the light. "I don't know what to think. I feel like my whole life has been a lie. What if my ex knew who I truly was and only married me to get my father's secrets and inherit his title? In fact, I'm sure that is exactly what happened. Edward was a nasty piece of work and a total playboy. Why else get married? Did his father know? Is that why I was hired to such a prestigious position and given to Edward as his PA for his departments? Is anything real?"

Montana was quiet as she considered what I'd said. I wondered what would have happened to me if I hadn't run into Laughlin. Maybe I'd be dead now. The thought made me shudder. I needed to change the subject, and I remembered how Montana had gotten out of sharing her back story with me.

"Hey!" she yelled as I splashed water on her.

"Come on, Montana, you need to tell me more about your *tough life*. Besides, I could really use the distraction, and I find you fascinating."

She gazed at me through one eye, shielding the other against the sun. "Fine, what do you want to know?"

I smiled at her open question. "Everything, of course. You left off by telling me you have three brothers, and one is a twin. You were raised by your eldest for the most part, because your father worked abroad. So, I'm guessing there is much more to the tale, because a father who works at a distance is not the definition of *tough* by the standards we established."

She glowed with mirth at my imitation of her saying the

word *tough*. "I like you, Suri; you're very different from anyone I have ever met. Did you know both Adam and I do yoga? In fact, he taught me, back when I was a teenager."

"Montana, you are such a shit and enviably an amazing conversationalist. Who taught you how to deflect like that?"

Now she broke down into peals of laughter, and I joined her. Her mirth was hard to resist, and I loved being with people who were so in the moment. "Let's just say that Eddy and I perfected it. I was a brat, and Eddy would help me lie to Ace, to keep me out of trouble. Eddy's been my best friend since I was very young. He was our neighbor growing up, and his parents still live in the same house where he grew up."

"I can't imagine being friends with anyone from my neighborhood growing up."

"Well, I suspect your neighborhood was a little more upper crust than mine." She took a swig from the wine cooler she held. "Grade nine year, we had a new student whom I made friends with and brought into our fold. She turned out to be a nasty piece of work." Montana stayed quiet, and I almost wondered if she'd fallen asleep. Whoever the new student was, she obviously had impacted Montana's young life.

Montana then went into great detail on how she met the new kid. "I was outside the school on our lunch break when Otter, my fellow bandmate and friend, came outside."

'Hey, everyone, have you met the new kid yet?' Otter asked as he joined the crew outside on the grass for our school lunch break.

'Who is he?' Alex yelled from the grass where Dillon had him in a headlock. Boys, *I thought and shook my head.* "Alex is my twin, and Dillon was a friend at the time."

'Not him, Alex, her—a really cute her. I invited her to come out and meet you guys, so be nice.' He said that to everyone but was looking at me when he said it. Then Otter gave us the scoop on Mercedes. She was a transfer student from a nearby suburb about forty minutes away, and her locker was right beside his,

which is why he knew of her already. A beautiful, partly Jamaican looking girl walked out and shyly made her way over to Otter, who was beaming and looking like a total idiot."

'Everyone, this is Mercedes.'

'Oh please,' she piped up. 'Mercy for short. Mercedes is too long of a name to be saying, so Mercy would be great.'

"We took turns introducing ourselves, but when she met Alex, her eyes lingered for a while, sizing him up and obviously liking what she saw. Unfortunately, Otter noticed also, and that created a rift right off the start. He tried directing her attention from Alex to me when he introduced me, by saying Alex and I were twins. I made the mistake of mentioning that we had two older brothers. Then she mumbled, *'Must be good looking if you two look like them.'*"

"Alex had blushed with the attention, and I had hoped for Otter's sake that Alex wouldn't date Mercy. He never did, but she didn't stop trying for a while, which set up another rift— between my best friend, who was in love with my brother, and our group's new member, putting me right in the middle."

I tried to imagine a twin to Montana and what her other brothers would look like. Her husband was handsome, with GQ good looks. "Sounds like teen angst to me."

She gazed at me, her eyes now twinkling with mischief. "You think so? Well, through the remainder of high school, that same girl dated my ex, got me in a shit ton of trouble, had me beaten up by a gang and hospitalized, with broken ribs and a concussion."

"What,?" I gasped. "How is that possible?"

Montana chuckled, but there was no mirth. "During this time, my boyfriend was killed, still an unsolved mystery, and my father died in an explosion, all before I graduated high school. If it hadn't been for Adam, I don't know what would have happened."

I paddled closer and took her hand. "I am so sorry,

Montana, that is horrendous. But I can't help thinking, with what was shared last night at the bonfire, if your father's accident was really an accident."

Her eyes widened in surprise. "I, ah, that is an excellent question, Suri. I need to tell the guys, and they need to investigate. What if all the crap that has happened to me is related to something bigger?"

I thought about it. "I don't know, maybe. Tell me more about this Mercedes person and your history with her."

She lay back on the mat. "It all seems silly now that I'm older, but at the time, it was everything to me. That first weekend that we met Mercy, we invited her to a beach party. Our thing was to find someone older to go to the liquor store and purchase a twenty-sixer of rum, then we would go to the local store and get a what we called Big Gulp—basically a huge plastic cup. Then we'd fill it halfway with Coke, and when we got to the beach, we would fill the rest with rum. That would last us the entire evening."

I shook my head. I had never done anything like that. I had been such a good girl, I was beginning to feel like I'd missed out.

"We used Big Gulp cups for two reasons. The cops patrolled the beaches, and with those cups, they never suspected us of drinking booze. And two, sometimes my brother Danny would join us. Being all of us but Eddy, Pat and Matt were only fifteen years old, it wasn't cool for him to catch us drinking. Anyway, we arrived at Bikini Beach around nine and hadn't been there long, when Mercy pulled out a joint and lit up. That was a bit of a shock, as none of us had tried drugs to my knowledge, and our school had a pretty strong anti-drug program. Although no one said anything, you could feel the tension. She held out the doobie to us all to see if anyone else wanted any."

'You know, Mercy,' I said, 'we don't do drugs. They're for losers, but

you go ahead, we'll watch.' "Not well said on my part, but I wanted to make my point and hopefully get her to stop."

'I would have never taken you for a chicken, Montana. You like everyone to think you're a badass, but that's okay. You have it your way. Just sit there like a good little girl and watch the real badass.'

"Now, all eyes were on me. I had a reputation for being tough, and not many people would talk to me the way she had. I wanted to beat the crap out of her and make her swallow her words. I looked at Alex, and he shook his head no —he knew what was going on in my mind. But clearly, the gauntlet had been thrown, and I had to do something."

'Okay, Mercy. I'll tell you what, hotshot, you drink down what's left in your cup in one minute flat, and I will smoke your joint with you. Deal?'

"I underestimated Mercy. She picked up her cup, took off the lid, showing everyone how much was left. As I mentioned, the cups were huge, and I thought there was no way she would down it. But she showed me up again by throwing back her head and chugging it down. Otter timed it to make sure she didn't cheat. At fifty seconds, she had done it, and I hated to admit it, but I was impressed. The girl had a gut of steel! It was my turn next, and she relit the joint and passed it to me. I took a small toke, as I didn't want to look like a total amateur by inhaling too much and coughing. No one said a word but watched us as we passed it back and forth between us. My trouble came when I was done with the joint and I was so thirsty and had finished my Big Gulp. Ralph was beside me, so I grabbed his drink and chugged it down."

I could feel myself getting lost. "Wait, who is Ralph again?"

"Ralph was my brother's best friend and the drummer for his band. We had been friends since I was six years old, grade one."

"Wow, you seem like you have a really close crew you can depend on."

Montana smiled. "There is a tiny core group that I would give my life for in a heartbeat. Some have passed on, however, like Ralph." She looked sad, more downtrodden, more so than a woman her age should be. "Later, when it was time to leave, I attempted to stand, and I ended up toppling over Ralph's lap. I was laughing so hard, I couldn't get up and remained there until Alex intervened. I stood, swaying in Alex's grasp. When he let go, I promptly fell down onto Ralph's lap. I was feeling brave and put my arms around him. He put his arms around me and smiled at me, looking amused at my silly, drunken antics."

'Gee, Ralph,' I said. 'Did I ever tell you that you're adorable? And I like the way you play the skins, too.'

'Uh-oh, Alex, Mo is pissed. What are we going to do with her?' Ralph had asked, looking super amused.

'She could stay at my house,' Mercy said.

"When I looked at her, Suri, I swear on my life, the girl had a demonic expression on her face. It totally freaked me out. I remember shivering and sending a look to my brother. Thankfully, he didn't take her up on her offer. Being the brat I am, I looked at Ralph and told him I could spend the night at his house and then winked at him with a leer. He laughed so hard, we both fell off the log."

'I should let Mercy have you,' Alex whispered in my ear. 'Now behave yourself. I'm taking you to Eddy's. You can sleep in the spare room.' Montana giggled as she finished her tale.

"I am finding it easy to see you at the beach on a log, loaded and teasing some poor boy. But I have to ask, did you drink often?"

Montana laughed. "Back then, as often as possible. I became a bit of a child alcoholic. Adam changed that, of course, along with most of my bad habits, but I didn't make it easy for him."

"Oh, and how did he do that exactly?"

Montana blushed furiously, and I wondered if, like myself, Adam drove home the point like Laughlin did with me, by taking me over his lap. "I take it you were hard to control?"

Montana rolled her eyes. "That is what Ace, my eldest brother, would say. Adam, bless his non-condemning heart, always said that Ace was why I was so hard to control. He said if Alex had been the eldest, I would have had a lot less drama."

"So, does that mean if Ace had been your twin, the blame would have balanced out better?"

Montana laughed so hard, she and her empty bottle fell into the pool. Her head bobbed a moment later, sputtering and laughing still.

"I'm told he was the brat before me, so yes, the blame game would have leveled out, but also Alex trusts me and my instincts, so he would have made less of an issue of things. Ace turned everything into an issue."

She walked back to the shore, plopping down on a lounger. I jumped into the water and followed her. Time had gone by so quickly, I was surprised when my phone pinged with a text from Laughlin.

"Come on, Mo, that was the one-hour warning for dinner, time for us to get cleaned up." She gave me a strange look. "What?"

"You called me Mo."

"And?"

"Nothing, but only my old tribe calls me that. It is refreshing to make a new friend who treats me like they have known me forever."

I smiled, and when we parted at the landing, I said, "To be continued."

Montana giggled. "I'll meet you bright and early at the lagoon tomorrow and tell you more."

"Why tomorrow? We haven't gone in the hot tub yet."

"Suri, you are like a dog on a bone, you know that? Okay, see you in a bit, and I'll leave the hot tub as to be determined. The guys may want to join us, and if they do, we will reconvene tomorrow." She saluted and headed down the hall to her and Adam's suite.

Chapter 18

Laughlin

"**D**eclan, have you found anything in the phone records the night Sir Robert died?" Geoff was hovering over Declan's shoulder, his presence adding urgency to Declan's fevered search.

"Aye," he said, spinning around in the office chair suddenly, almost banging into Geoff. "Loc, did yer father say anything to you about having a man, undercover, inside the SOG group?"

"No, he didn't. His story to me was he was investigating something for the Order. A rumor about another location in Palestine. He left, I presumed to Palestine and, three days later, was found dead."

"But he never landed in Palestine," Geoff added. "You can tell that the flight manifest has been doctored." He placed it on the table, and the five of us huddled around and took a look.

"See this," Geoff pointed. "And look at this," he said, now placing down another form that had the flights from the Edinburgh airport. "This shows your father never flew that day." But he put down another sheet. "When you look here, you can see he flew out of Perth—"

"Perth? That airfield has been closed... since your father's disappearance," Geoff interrupted.

"For some reason, he flew from a different airport, and I hadn't known it—"

"Is it possible," Geoff interrupted, "that your father was trying to keep you safe and maybe whoever is responsible was more than happy to leave well enough alone. Then you started digging, and out of nowhere, Suri shows up. Perhaps the powers that be got worried."

I looked up at Declan. "Tell us about this undercover in the SOG. Who is he?"

"You know him, or at least Suri has seen him. The man on the beach in Turkey was your father's inside man, a deadly assassin, not a historian. That is why he was about to be assassinated. He knew too much."

My head was reeling with this new information. Marc had said the man had been taken in and placed in our relocation program. "Do you know where he is now? I was told he was moved into the witness protection program."

"Who told ye that, Loc? The man is dead. Ask yourself, why would someone from our Order, doing undercover work, be dead if he was under our protection, aye?"

I thought back to my conversation with Marc. He'd spearheaded the intel for me as my second, and no one knew my plans better than he had. I had trusted him with my life, with everything. Could he be the traitor?

Just then, there was a knock on the door. My maid, Annie, opened the door. "Just letting you know dinner will be ready in an hour, sir. Would you gentlemen like any pre-dinner refreshments?"

"A round of scotch, please, Annie." She nodded and left

on her errand. When I looked back at the men, still huddled around the table, they wore identical expressions. "What? Why are you all looking at me like that?"

Geoff took the lead. "How many staff members do you have, Laughlin? And how many have access to this room?"

That took me back, as I was just attempting to come to terms with my best and only friend being the culprit.

A moment later, Annie knocked on the door and delivered a tray with a crystal decanter filled with Scotch and five crystal goblets. I poured, and we sat down, taking a reprieve.

"Listen, you need to look at those closest to you. I had a maid, very dedicated, and she had access to my private office for cleaning purposes. Montana had an attempt on her life while she was staying with my wife and me. Adam was away on business, as were both her elder brothers. There had been attempts made on her life already, and both Ace and Adam were concerned, so I had her come to me."

I caught a glimpse of deep remorse on Geoff's face before it disappeared.

"My fiancée, at the time, died that night, Laughlin, or I should say she was dead for a few seconds before her twin was able to pull her back," Adam said.

I was about to ask what happened when Geoff once again took over. "My housekeeper, turned out, was a little crazy—split personality. Add to that her obsession with Adam, and a big payout from Montana's nemesis was enough for her to let in the assassin and join him in murder."

I chugged back my scotch, refilled my glass and chugged that too.

"Jesus… your personal staff was in on the deal. Well-vetted too, I assume?"

Geoff smiled, but it didn't reach his eyes. "Yes, my staff was chosen by me personally and had extensive background checks. Eddy here found sealed records on Bridget. She had a record of stalking her victims."

I glanced at Adam. When he was not shuttered, his eyes were much older, very much like Montana. I had no doubt being the golden boy and Mason title inheritor and her husband had given him some early life experiences he would rather have done without.

"There were signs," Adam added, looking at me. "I missed them or chose to ignore them. So, Laughlin, you need to look at your staff with new eyes. Eddy doesn't have the connections in Britain that he has in Canada, but Declan does. He can provide you with everything you need, as long as you provide him with a place to start."

I nodded my head, wondering why someone as well trained as I had overlooked the obvious place to begin a search in one's own house. "Don't beat yourself up, Lord Roswell," Geoff said with a smirk. "The best of us miss the most obvious sometimes. At heart, I believe we all want to know we have trustworthy people working for us."

He was right. I sighed and plunked my glass down on the tray. "I will lock the office while we are at dinner, but to ensure we are indeed secure, Eddy, can you set up surveillance in here?"

"Easy enough, I will change the coding on your surveillance equipment and have your cameras aimed inside while we are at dinner. We can come back afterward and look through the footage and finish up for the night."

Half an hour later, we headed to the dining room for dinner. My heart was heavy and hoped Annie and the rest of my staff, all who were with my father as well, were trustworthy. And then there was Marc. He had the information to pull off everything that had happened so far. If digging into my staff didn't answer who the mole was, he would be the one we investigated next.

Chapter 19

Suri

L aughlin was quiet at dinner. Whatever the guys were working on had been unsettling for him. He took my hand and held it during our meal, making eating difficult, but as he obviously needed to feel me, I had no complaints.

Everyone, including Eddy's men, was seated while Thor's men took over the patrol, affording our guests some downtime. Adam seemed as morose as Laughlin, and I wondered what had been shared to affect both men.

The lord of the manor did his best to be a grateful host, but Laughlin was no social butterfly at the best of times. So, taking the lead, I told some stories from when I was in my dream job in Boston fundraising.

"Did you put on the Children of the World Benefit, for Wealthco's head office in Boston about three years ago?" Geoff inquired.

"You were there, Standford Construction Inc.. I remember now; you were on the guest list, but I thought you didn't come." I was shocked by how small the world indeed was. I'd found out that Montana, Declan, and I all shared a distant relation, and now I find out that I knew Geoff in my old life.

"I was late and a personal guest of Stanhope the first. I, of course, am much younger but met Edward when I was just starting out. Back then, Wealthco was much smaller and worked in only North America. I liked him, but not his son, and unfortunately, I have also met your ex, Suri, Edward the third, or junior as how I refer to him. A total ass wipe if you ask me."

I don't know what I was expecting but certainly not so frank a statement, and it broke through the awkwardness of the evening. "Touché, Geoff, ass wipe would describe him perfectly."

"Sounds like Matt. Remember Eddy, he was one of your buds back in the day."

Eddy laughed. "Well, yeah, I remember, of course. Montana was always dating older boys back in the day.

Adam grinned. "And here I thought I was the only older boy she'd ever dated."

That started some good-natured ribbing between Adam and Eddy, who teased Montana mercilessly until dessert and coffee arrived. I was almost envious of how close the three of them were, and Geoff seemed amused, dropping in comments here and there.

It turned out that Adam was almost twenty when he started dating the nearly sixteen-year-old Montana. And because she had no parents, Geoff's wife had been like a den mother to all of Montana's brothers and their girlfriends and friends over the years.

When we finally wrapped it up, even Laughlin seemed more relaxed than I'd seen him in days. The light bantering had been a good distraction for him and the rest. I grew up with one sister I was not very close to, and Laughlin had been an only child.

I wondered if watching the three of them made him wish he'd had a larger family. "I must admit, I am a little envious of the closeness you all share. It is inspiring."

"Yeah, I used to feel sorry for Adam, being an only child, but he said he liked having three brothers, so I stopped," Montana said as she looked into Adam's eyes.

"Well, lads, I do believe we have a little more work to get done. Ladies, we'll see you later." We stood, and Laughlin pulled me in tight. "I want you, Suri. Just looking at you makes me hard."

"Mm, well, I don't feel bad about that, as it is nice to be wanted."

"What are you two going to get up to?"

"I promised Montana hot tub time."

"Be careful, Suri. I don't think you have anything to worry about, but don't trust anyone, not even my staff." I wanted to ask why, but he kissed me on the forehead and told me he'd fill me in later if their suspicions turned out to be true.

Half an hour later, Montana and I were in the hot tub. The night was beautiful, with a crystal-clear sky overhead. I was ready to hear more of her story and turned off the hard jets, creating a more peaceful atmosphere.

"Okay, queen of distraction, time to carry on. You were telling me about your nemesis and the first time you met her. When did you know she was going to be an ongoing problem?"

"The night Alex and the band were playing the Halloween dance, thanks to moi," she said, pointing at herself. "In the early days, I co-wrote and made the bookings. Anyway, back then, the dance was an opportunity to get heard, so the guys played. That night, my brother Alex finally took notice of my best friend. And Mercy, who'd been trying to gain his attention, was pissed. Later, she showed up at our beach party with my ex-boyfriend Matt, the guy we were talking about at dinner. Danny had caught word of the party and was joining us. He was friends with Matt and Eddy and another friend of all of us, Pat. That was a problem when we hung in the same social circles. But everyone agreed to keep quiet regarding the alcohol, and we hoped Danny would never guess. In traditional West End style, we bought Big Gulps for our rum. With Danny already there, Alex and I disappeared to fill up our cups with rum. Adam strolled by, and I held a finger against my lips in a shh fashion, and he just grinned and kept on walking."

She paused for a moment, as if thinking back. "We sat in a circle formation, and I had Adam on one side of Alex and me on the other. Opposite us, sat Matt and Mercy. I was able to ignore Mercy and enjoy Adam's company. We discussed literature and art, two of my favorite topics. Kind of weird, actually, as most kids wouldn't consider it cool. Anyway, it became apparent throughout the evening that Adam and I shared many interests. Adam talked about some of his goals, and I found it refreshing to speak to a person who had plans for their future. When I glanced at the others, I noticed that Matt was staring at me and Mercy was giving sidelong glances to Alex. Adam took note of the animosity from across the fire and asked me about Mercy and Matt. When I had filled him in, he said that explained why she was glaring at me. I shifted my focus to her and saw that horrible, evil look I had seen that first time we had been at the beach together, and Adam saw it, too."

Montana stopped there, and I processed her words. It sounded to me like her coveted position in her tribe had created an enemy.

"Her hatred for me grew from that night. As I mentioned earlier, she orchestrated a gang beating several months later, and I ended up in the hospital for a few days. I'd had a hissy fit at a party, where I learned my brother Ace was getting married, and I knew nothing about it. I got hammered and stumbled home, but on the way, I got jumped by Mercy and a few others. Eddy found me at the side of the road and took me to the hospital."

"I'm having a hard time relating. I have never been beaten up or broken anything. Muscle strain from too much yoga is the extent of my injuries."

Montana smiled. "Keep it that way. Being a badass is overrated."

"If you don't mind me saying so, you seem to have a lot of scars, battle wounds?"

She nodded. "This one messed me up for close to a year." She turned and showed me a two-inch long scar beside her spine.

"What's that from?"

"Mercy and I fought in an alley, and I won. When I turned my back to leave, she stabbed me."

"Can I touch it?" She looked puzzled but nodded. I placed my hand over her scar, using Reiki to feel the extent of the scar tissue that she must have. I had begun to notice that sometimes the Reiki energy was more challenging than other times to access. I assumed it was because of my headspace, but I was starting to realize it was based on the recipient's need.

In this case, energy hummed down my arms and through my hands rapidly and poured into Montana. She lay her head down on her arms at the side of the hot tub, completely surrendering to the energy. As my arms heated and the energy funneled, I found I could see the injury from the inside.

In my mind's eye, what had happened was as clear as if I was witnessing it. I could see the dark energy in the wound inflicted by hate. It was almost tangible, a black hate-filled vapor. Instinctively, I began to pull my hands from her spine, one after the other, like pulling a rope. I continued until I felt all of the black vapor dissipate. When I finished, Montana opened one eye and regarded me. She was so relaxed, I was afraid she'd slump into the hot tub and drown. "Montana, are you okay?"

"I feel amazing, but I'm suddenly so weak, I just want to sleep. Can you call Adam for me? I think I need help."

I was worried. Maybe I had done too much at once. I called Laughlin and asked him to send Adam out to the hot tub. I assured him all was well, but two minutes later, both Adam and Declan arrived, took one look at her, and both sets of eyes moved to me.

"I, uh, did some energy work and, well, she is, well, she told me she suddenly felt exhausted. I'm sorry, I was trying to help."

Declan lifted Montana out of the hot tub like she weighed nothing.

"Suri, I feel drunk with good vibes. You're a powerful woman, thank you." Then she snuggled into the giant Scot's chest and fell asleep.

"I'll carry her up for ye, Adam," Declan said, already making his way for the house. Adam's gaze shifted to me, his eyes boring into mine, and I swore the man could see souls. "Thank you, Suri. I haven't seen her that relaxed in a very long time. How did you do it?"

"It's called Reiki. Montana was telling me about Mercy and then showed me her scar on her back. I just felt compelled to touch it, and I'm glad I did. There was some real darkness still in there, reciprocal bad energy. I guess this Mercy person truly hates Montana."

"Hated—she's dead now. That's another long story, but I'll let her tell you. She hadn't made a new friend since I met her when she was fifteen. I think your friendship could be a balm for her troubled soul. Montana takes on the world with a ferocity that I've rarely ever seen and not in a woman, at least not in my lifetime. I see her as a Boudicca, a fierce female warrior. But she takes too much to heart and blames herself for all the crap that went down because of the angst between her and Mercy, and she shouldn't."

I felt this man's pain and love for his wife. What an incredible partnership they were, and I wondered if Laughlin and I could ever be as close as these two.

Adam smiled then. "This is my first time meeting Laughlin, and I can tell he's got some pain of his own. Maybe you can wield your miracle Reiki on him."

I smiled. "Maybe, I'll give it a try, and Adam," I said as he turned to leave, "thank you for sharing with me. I appreciate it. As a yogi and a healer, I try to help where I can. I guess what I'm saying is I hope our friendship is not regulated by circumstances. I really like you and Montana. You're good people."

He smiled and gave me a warm, one-armed hug like one does when they're being friendly but don't want anything misconstrued. "Thank you, Suri, we like you too."

Then he walked away and into the house, and I was left to ponder all I had learned and seen for myself.

Chapter 20

Laughlin

I had followed Declan and Adam to the patio but stayed back as they made their way to the hot tub. Adam's wife was slumped over, and I assumed she had overheated from too much warmth and booze—the woman could drink.

Declan carried her back, and when he passed me, I noticed Montana was asleep with a small smile curving her lips. " She's fine, just fell asleep." He kept going, and I turned my attention back to outside. Suri was talking to Adam, and I could see her eyes shining from here. They did that when she was inspired or feeling love. I felt my hands tighten into fists when he leaned in and gave her a hug. Jealousy surged through me like a pulsing beast. I would kill him when he walked through the door.

But Adam stopped and gazed at me in that soulful way of his. "You have quite a woman there, Laughlin. She has healed a wound in my wife, and I am very grateful." He gripped my arm in a bond of brotherhood, releasing all the tension in me from a moment ago.

He left; I assumed to go check in on his wife. I turned my gaze back outside in time to see all the lights suddenly go out. That was odd. No maintenance checks were scheduled for this late at night. "Suri?" No answer. "Suri!" I was louder this time, and the desperation I was feeling was evident in my voice.

I stepped outside, tuning my senses to the environment. I was trained for whatever was out there. With the lights off outside but on inside, it was hard to see into the shadows. I looked to where I'd last seen Suri, standing by the hot tub, her gaze set on the lagoon. Had she decided to go for a swim to cool off?

I listened but heard no splashing sounds and wondered if she was meditating. Suddenly, Eddy appeared at my side. He motioned to a corner beyond the hot tub, a particularly dark spot allotted for privacy. Suri wasn't there, but a rustling sound drew our attention.

Eddy motioned for me to skirt around to the left while he took a right. He already had Steve and Mike making their way around the back. When we charged the bush, it was to find Thor tied up, his mouth gagged, and a note pinned to his shirt.

"Give me everything, or she joins your father in the grave."

My heart froze, and it was that moment when I realized I truly loved Suri. I would tear the entire world apart to get her back.

Eddy's phone tinged. "It's all clear; no one is here, but all of Laughlin's guards are down, drugged by the looks of it."

"Set up a perimeter. I'll get Steve and Mike to bring in the men. Maybe when they wake up, someone can tell us what happened."

"Roger that."

"Luke, Rob, and J2 are setting up a perimeter. All of your guys are out, drugged by the looks of things. Steve and Mike will bring them in, and we can get a briefing when they wake up. Let's go check the video footage. We must be able to see something that will give us a clue."

I nodded, but I wondered if Marc had anything to do with this. Pulling out my phone, I sent my 'friend' a text: *Need you; come now.*

My phone pinged immediately with: *On my way.*

"Eddy, let your men know that a friend, Lord Marcus, is on his way, and I want him allowed entry." He nodded, and I lifted Thor, throwing the large man over my shoulders in a herculean effort, and carried him inside.

Back in my headquarters office, I dropped Thor onto the couch. "Laughlin, we were right about your staff. Come and look at this," Geoff called.

I moved over to the monitors and watched as my maid, |Annie, descended the stairs and punched in the code to enter my private office. She then removed that painting on the wall that hid the master switches for the property, security, locks, and lights. I wracked my brain, trying to think if I had ever given her the code to my room or shown her where the panel was.

"Looks like we found our conspirator."

A knock at the door announced Marc's arrival. When I opened the door and beckoned him in, he took in the scene before him with wide eyes. "I take it something has gone amiss?"

"It has," I conceded," and if you don't convince me of your innocence, then prepare for more than *something* to go amiss, like your life."

Marc looked genuinely shocked, then offended, and then hurt. Long before he uttered the words, I knew he was innocent. I had been trained in interrogation techniques, and no one could fake what had spontaneously occurred with his expressions.

"Marc, you know Geoff. This is his son and second, Adam

Northrop. Eddy, his head of security and private detective." Marc shook hands with both men and then turned to Declan. "This is Declan Campbell."

"The Flying Scotsman, Declan Campbell?"

Declan grinned ferally. "In the flesh, Lord Marcus. Now maybe you would like to tell us where the lass is."

"Lass, what lass?"

I let Declan take over. He had trained with Eddy and became head of security for Montana's vast musical empire with her brother. Added to that, his skill set and death combats made him the deadliest person in the room.

Declan's demeanor became ice as he stalked menacingly towards Marcus. He grabbed him by the collar and dropped him onto a chair in front of the monitor, replaying the scene with Annie. "How much did ye pay her to turn off the lights? Who are you working with? Who knocked out Laughlin's men?"

Marcus was Templar trained. He wouldn't roll over and wet himself because the intimidating Declan Campbell posed a threat. But his shock was evident; he knew nothing, and we all knew it.

Declan suddenly slapped him on the back. "Good to know you're one of us, welcome."

Declan's demeanor shifted so quickly that Marc was still in shock. Finally, his gaze lifted to me. "What the bloody hell is going on here, Laughlin?"

"Suri has been kidnapped."

"Well, I'd say before you lose your chance, you may want to go looking for that maid. Clearly, she is guilty of something."

I was so caught up in the scene unfolding before me, I had forgotten that Annie was somehow complicit in what had happened to Suri.

"Already caught," Eddy confirmed. "She was about to

make her escape through the kitchen, but she was caught by J2. He's bringing her here now."

The door flew open, and in came J2 with a protesting Annie. When she saw the screen, she blanched. She was guilty, and now she knew that lying would get her nowhere.

"It's not what you think, Laughlin."

"Really? And what does it look like, Annie? Because, to me, it looks like you helped someone kidnap my girlfriend. How does it look to you?"

J2 deposited Annie in a chair, then he shared a few words privately with Eddy and left.

Annie dropped her gaze, fumbling nervously with her fingers. I didn't have time for this shit; I needed to find Suri. I pulled a total dominant move, not something I had ever done outside the bedroom. I gripped Annie by the hair so tight, she yelped. "Tell me where Suri is, or I will end your life right bloody now. Do you understand?"

Tears rolled down her cheeks, but I wasn't letting up. The air in the room had gone deathly still. They knew I would do what I threatened.

"It is John Smith who has your lass."

"Who the hell is John Smith? Tell me, now!"

"He's your half-brother."

I let go of her hair so quickly, her head snapped back. I stepped away and looked at Marc. "Do you know what she is talking about?" But he didn't; I could see it in his eyes. The shock I found there was probably as apparent as my own.

"I don't have any brothers."

Annie was crying in earnest now, and I felt like the world was tilting.

"Annie, I don't have any brothers, half or otherwise."

"But you do, sir, not the one who died at birth, but the one your father had with his mistress. He was born a few months before ye, Laughlin, and has come to claim your father's legacy."

My rage resurfacing, I again gripped her hair and craned her neck, so she had no choice but to look up at me. "Why have you never told me? If you knew, how come I am just hearing about this now?"

She swallowed the lump from her throat. "Because John Smith is my son. I had an affair with your father, and as a result, we had a son."

I again let go suddenly, my hand feeling like it was burnt. "You?"

Declan stepped in again. "Lass, you'd better tell us the entire story and quickly. Time is of the essence."

Annie nodded and seemed relieved with unburdening her secret. But could we trust her?

"Okay, lass, start from the beginning." Declan crossed his arms, waiting for Annie to spill.

"Laughlin's father had an arranged marriage. He was fond of his wife, but they had no passion between them. She was older and set in her ways, and I was young and inexperienced. I was flattered by the attention that was paid to me by Mr. Roswell."

She paused to take a sip of water that Marc had handed to her. She shakily placed her glass down, sat back, and let out a long breath, then she continued her story. "When I became pregnant, I was so happy. I was stupid, thinking that Robert would want a child he could never claim as his heir. When I told him the news, he was furious and told me to have an abortion."

She took a shuddering breath. "I refused, hoping he'd come around. He never did, and when my baby was born, he took him away from me. I never even got to hold him." Annie began to cry in earnest now, and if her story was to be believed, then my father was a monster.

"I thought he was dead, that Robert had him killed. But he wasn't. He was given to a well-off family and raised in a good home. Mr. Roswell paid the family a yearly allowance to ensure that John had everything he needed and then some. All this, of course, I just found out recently."

She gazed up at me with remorse in her eyes. "I thought you two could have been brothers. I thought your life would have been less lonely." She turned her head back to the room. "Somehow, John put two and two together. It was he who killed yer father, Lord Robert. I'm sorry, Laughlin."

"But I thought my father was on a mission for the Order?"

"Aye, he was, but when he got wind of John causing trouble, he went to deal with him on his way to the airport. John said that Lord Robert tried to kill him, and in defending himself, he killed him instead. He wants revenge on Laughlin and what he calls his rightful inheritance. When your father died, nothing was mentioned in the will about John or me, and he was furious. Now he wants to take your place and become the next Lord of Roswell."

"Why didn't you ever leave, Annie?" I asked softly, wondering why a woman who had been so abused would stay in a place that held bad memories.

"Because I thought that maybe one day your father and I would, you know, marry. He loved me in his own strange way; of that I am certain. When Robert died so suddenly, I didn't want to leave you by yourself. You seemed so lost in yourself and in your pain. I couldn't do it."

"Then John showed up, and everything changed?"

"Aye, I didn't believe him at first, but he looks a lot like you, Laughlin, more like your father than you, even. Then he told me how he found out, and I knew he was my son. At first, he convinced me how wronged I was, and then he convinced me to help him take you down. But it was hard, because you care about nothing. Then the lass came along, and John said it was time to strike."

Thor had awakened from his drug inducement and asked if Annie had a picture of John.

"Nay, but you do. You hired him right after Laughlin asked you to increase security."

"I never hired a John Smith," Thor negated.

Annie smiled sadly. "I know; you hired Sir Henry Fitzwilliam's son, Malcolm Fitzwilliam. That is John."

I felt my blood turn to ice in my veins. "Annie, do you know how John found out about his true identity?"

"He said he saw him once, with Henry Fitzwilliam, his guardian, and it all came together. He questioned Henry, but he didn't reveal the truth, only confirmed it after John had done the research and confirmed who his parents were."

I was fuming. My father had given the baby to his best friend, to keep safe and keep his secret. Henry knew and made up some bullshit about a baby brother who died at birth, taking my mother with him.

"Annie, do you know how my mother died?" I braced myself, knowing I wouldn't like her answer.

"She killed herself, and you found her body. I'm sorry, Laughlin. Your father threatened my life if I told anyone, and well, then, it's been so long, I never thought about it again."

Alice's words came back to me, and then so did the memories. Along with my father convincing me, my mother had too much medicine and had gone to sleep. He hadn't lied, but he manipulated the truth. My fear of love wasn't love. It was abandonment. If I got Suri back, when I got Suri back, I corrected myself, I would marry the lass and make her mine.

"Annie, is John determined to take out his anger on me and mine? Or do you think we could come to a compromise?"

She looked puzzled at my question. "I'm asking if he is determined to kill Suri or me if he doesn't get what he wants, or would he be happy with half of my father's inheritance. Share it with me and come out of the dark and into the light? I will acknowledge him as my brother, as he should have been from the beginning."

Of course, I would make my statement more for her benefit than an actual belief that John would let Suri go, but it was worth a try. Then another possibility entered my mind and one that made more sense.

"He expected you to get caught, didn't he? You were meant to be a buffer to help him achieve his goal. Murder is not on his mind at all, is it? In fact, I would wager that this story is the reverse. You are the one who found out the secret that John is still alive. You went looking for him and no doubt offered yourself to Henry to get the information you sought. Why wouldn't the best friend of a powerful lord know of the birth of a baby?"

Annie's soft brown eyes went hard with hate. "Well, aren't you your father's son? That's right, and now John has your precious Suri, and if I don't leave here alive, he will slice her throat."

I wondered if she had always been psychotic or if events with my father had thrown her off the deep end.

"But don't you want your son, John, to get all he deserves?" Geoff stepped up and took her hand in his. "Surely, you would rather John be rich and you the lady of the house like you always dreamed," he continued.

Annie was buying it, her nasty leer changing to sheer arrogance. "That's right, just like we deserve. I should have been queen, not that nasty cold fish Robert kept in his bed, just because she had the correct name. A Sinclair, just like the snotty bitch you brought home. Did you really think I would tolerate another gold-digging whore in my house?" She was screaming the words as if my father was still in the room.

Eddy motioned me out of the room while Geoff kept

talking in soothing tones to Annie. "Laughlin, you need to call this Fitzwilliam fellow and see if he can find out where Suri is. We have to assume that your half-brother is as crazy as his mother."

Marc joined us. "Let me, Loc. I know Fitzwilliam as well as you, and I need to do something to help."

I nodded at my friend and hoped he'd forgive me when this was over. Marc pulled out his phone and called, putting it on speaker. "Hello, Henry, this is Lord Marcus. How are you?"

"Oh, Marc, lovely, and yourself?"

"Well, I have a situation here, Henry. I have a raving housemaid who is claiming that you have been housing the illegitimate half-brother of my good friend Laughlin, Lord of Roswell."

Dead silence from the other end.

"Henry, your ward has kidnapped Laughlin's woman. His mother is threatening to have her throat slit. I suggest you tell us where he is keeping her."

"Don't hurt him. He's a good lad. I don't know what Annie has been filling his head with, but I promise you, this is all her, and he is doing her bidding."

"To be determined, Henry, but if Suri is harmed in any way, I can't be responsible for what Laughlin will do."

Again, dead silence on the other end.

"How about you find your wayward adopted son and tell him we'll make a trade. In half an hour, his mother for Suri."

I was about to speak, but Marc silenced me.

"I will find him. Where should we meet?" Henry asked.

"Roswell Abbey, see you in half an hour, and she'd better be unharmed, Henry."

Marc hung up the phone and looked at Eddy. "Okay, what's the plan?"

Chapter 21

Suri

I was deep in thought about Montana and her wounds when I heard a whisper of movement behind me. "I hope she is all right," I said without looking, assuming it was Laughlin behind me. But instead of his powerful arms wrapped around me, a cloth was put over my face and a horrible smelling odor overwhelmed my senses, knocking me out.

When I came to, I was tied to a chair in a dank space. Having been in the hot tub in my bikini, I was freezing. I blinked my eyes open and took in the darkness. I was in a root cellar or underground storage I assumed, by the smell and the cold.

I tried moving, but both my arms and ankles were tied. What the hell had happened? Was I kidnapped again? A flash of being tied down on a bed invaded my consciousness, and everything I'd tried so hard to push away from the past came barreling in, an onslaught of images, and then the reel of horror began to play out, and there was nothing I could do about it.

My hands were tied to each post, as were my feet. I should have been terrified. But this seemed to be a game, an unwanted one but a game all the same. I was angry instead of fearful.

"Edward," I yelled. "Edward! God damn it, Edward, get your ass in here and untie me this instant."

The door creaked open, and there stood Edward, leaning against the doorjamb with a drink in hand. "Hello, sweetness, did you have a good time?"

"Edward. Untie me at once. I have to go back. I have things to finish. When I come home tomorrow, we can play, okay?" As I spoke, he had been slowly moving towards me. He was standing directly over me now. "Edward, untie me, please. Now!"

That got his attention. He put down his drink and took the loose end of the rope from where he'd tied my hands and looped it around my neck and retied it. Now, if I tried to struggle, I'd be virtually hanging myself. Then, he ripped open my clothes. He picked up his drink and tossed it on me. I screamed. What was this? He leaned over and began to lap up the whiskey he had dumped on my chest and stomach.

"You know you are ruining everything, don't you, Mary? All you had to do was be a good girl and do as I say. Now you are thinking for your-self, and that just won't do."

Was he serious? Holy shit, I was in trouble. I was about to scream when he slapped my face so hard that I was too stunned to do anything, the rope around my neck tightening. Then he ripped my panties off and stuffed them in my mouth. "You will remain tied to this bed until you learn your place in this world, my world. Nod if you understand."

My only response was to glare.

He must be drunk, *I rationalized. This wasn't him. Or was it? My legs had been tied spread-eagled and he was undoing his suit pants. My eyes were wide as I watched him undress, getting ready to mount me against my will. My own husband was about to rape me. Holy hell.*

I started to buck, trying to delay the inevitable. Edward laughed as he slapped my face repeatedly. He picked up his pants, slowly drew his belt out of the loops and swished it through the air, then he began to land it on my exposed thighs and stomach. I was terrified, the pain increasing my fear. I stopped moving, hoping my obedience would make him stop.

"That's better," he cooed, "See? Now, how hard was that? Just me and you, Mary. And I will be me, and we will go back to being the Comcost power couple we were meant to be. Well. At least a power couple. You see, Mary, while you were off learning to bend your hot body into fancy new poses for me to fuck, I have been fired from motherfucking Comcost. Stupid assholes needed a fall guy for all the illegal dealings we were doing, and it turns out... I was it. But they will pay Mary. Mark my words, they will pay!"

Now I understood. Something big had happened while I was away, and he hadn't shared it with me. My phone call must have pushed him over the edge. What an idiot I was. I should have engaged with him first, to see where his headspace was.

Another lesson learned. I would have to tread carefully. Edward stared out the window, his only movement the small circles of his drink hand swooshing its contents around. I made enough noise to get his attention, and he pulled my panties out of my mouth.

"You have something to say, sweetness?"

"Edward, I'm sorry I wasn't here for you, but I am now. Please untie me and tell me everything that happened. Maybe I can help."

He smiled then, the old George Clooney smile he used to give me in those first few months we were together. Then his expression went through several disturbing shifts, ending with a wicked smile that left me covered in goosebumps.

"No, Mary. You will stay as you are. And I will have my way with you until you see that your new insights weren't insights at all. That wasn't you, but a possible version of you. This is the real you. In my bed, at my disposal, and nothing else is acceptable."

"But, Edward, I may forgive you when you realize what you've done and try to apologize for it. Others won't be so lenient. My group knows I'm missing. They will wonder what happened to me."

He leaned over the bed like he was going to kiss me and then slapped me again. "What do you take me for, a fool? They won't be looking for you, Mary. I spoke with Stacey. She believes there has been a death in the family, and you had to fly out of town. By the time they realize what has occurred, it will be too late."

"Too late for what, Edward?"

"Too late for you, sweetness. For me. For us. We will both be dead. You see... I mean to kill you... and then... I'm going to kill my mother-fucking self."

I was sobbing at the horrific memory when I heard a door open and a shard of light appeared. At first, I thought it was Laughlin. The man who entered the room was the same height and similar build, not quite as big. I squinted up to his face, the light behind him slightly blinding me.

"Don't cry at my expense, Suri. I'm sure my brother will come through, and you will be free to go."

"I'm sorry, I don't know what you're talking about. Who is your brother?"

He grinned, but his smile was anything but happy. He seemed like an unhappy soul, and despite my situation, I felt sorry for him.

"Lord Roswell, of course. Laughlin is my brother, or half-brother. If he hasn't told you, he will soon. My mother will confess to him, as she planned, and then he will do anything to get you back." He moved closer to me and gripped my hair, pulling my head back at a sharp angle. I cringed but otherwise held still and said nothing.

"Of course, if he doesn't, I may keep you for myself. You are just my taste, strong but soft, voluptuous, a perfect figure, really. You remind me of a brunette Marilyn Monroe." He let go of my hair, leaving a deep throb in my skull.

"May I ask your name?" I asked tentatively. Being kidnapped by Edward had taught me a lot; mostly, don't spook the monster.

He grinned at me, and again, it did not reach his eyes. "You may, but I will not answer." I was about to ask for water when I heard thumping from above and then someone calling for "Malcolm." He swore under his breath and left me, closing the door and sealing me in the dark.

Fifteen minutes later, he was back and untying the rope around my wrists, then tying them again in front of me. He untied my ankles and pulled me to my feet. "We're going for a quick ride, Suri. Don't try to fight me or run, understand?"

I remained silent, only nodding my head.

He dragged me up the stairs and, waiting for us, was an older man, shorter with kind eyes and a balding head. "You must be Suri. I'm sorry about all of this, Suri. I promise you that this is very uncharacteristic of Malcolm."

Malcolm glared at the man. "Quiet; she doesn't need to know anything about me, Father." So, this was the father.

"Please help me, I—"

Before I could utter another word, John tied a cloth around my mouth. Then he marched me out a door and into a vehicle, the older gentleman following and getting into the passenger seat.

"Malcolm, all we have to do is trade her for your mother, and nothing will happen. You'll be free. They just want the lass back."

Malcolm didn't respond, but from my angle, the resolute expression he wore told me he wasn't interested in being free but in something else.

Wherever we were going, the ride was short, maybe ten minutes long. When we arrived, I was blindfolded and then helped out of the car. I walked as best I could with a man on either side, feeling dense foliage under my feet and then cement.

"Hold it right there," I heard someone who sounded like Eddy yell.

We stopped walking, and the older man, Malcolm's father, left my side. "I don't have a weapon. I just wish to speak with my godson, Laughlin."

Godson? Oh dear, this was getting messy. But I understood the expression Malcolm wore now. He had nothing to lose but everything to gain. He wanted an inheritance, I was sure of it. I began to wonder what Laughlin would give up to get me back. I didn't like the idea of being used for this half-brother's gain.

I tried pulling loose, but the man's grip was iron, and he increased it. I was sure that I would have finger bruises on my arm.

Then I heard a shrill woman's voice ring out, "Malcolm, kill the bitch; kill his good for nothing wife and take your rightful place."

I was confused and wished I wasn't wearing a blindfold. Then I heard the slight rustle to my left and moved my feet to create enough sound to hopefully hide the gentle rustle. Someone was sneaking up from behind. I continued to shuffle my feet and then heard a *thwack* sound.

A moment later, the blindfold was removed, and I saw my rescuer, Laughlin.

"Thank god you're all right, lass." He quickly undid my binds and pulled me in tight. Around me, there was action. What it was, I didn't care. I was safe, rescued by my personal Templar Knight.

I began to sob. I don't know why, from the relief, I guess, but mostly gratefulness that I was not collateral damage.

"It's okay now, Suri. I'm sorry, so sorry this happened to you." He held me back and looked into my eyes. His were unreadable. "Suri, if you give me another chance, I promise, nothing like this will ever happen again. I love you, Suri, and I want to spend the rest of my life proving to you how much."

"I love you too, Laughlin."

He scooped me up and carried me to the car. He continued to hold me while Thor drove us back to the castle. When we arrived, he took me to our room, filling the tub with hot water, Epsom salts, and some flower oil. Then he dipped me into its warm embrace. He left and came back a moment later with a bottle of water and painkillers.

The shivering ebbed, and I lay back, exhausted. "Laughlin, before we decide forever, there is something I need to tell you."

"I'm sure whatever it is, lass, can wait until tomorrow."

"Please, it really can't."

Laughlin got undressed and sat opposite me in the giant tub, allowing me to see his handsome face without having to crane my neck

I told Laughlin my entire story with Edward. Up until this point, I had made vague references to our marriage. I said to him that Edward was dead but not the steps leading to that moment.

"Laughlin, tonight, when I was tied up in the dark, it all came flooding back, and it was so real. I had been pushing it away, but I thought I had shelved it because I was over it. The truth is everything that happened was like a trigger, and I was terrified."

He smiled indulgently. "I understand, and even if you were truly over it, Suri, what you experienced still would have been a trigger. Trauma will do that, and I'm sorry it happened on my watch. I vow that nothing like this will ever happen again."

"What happens now, Laughlin, with Malcolm?"

"He and Henry are with Geoff, Thor, and Eddy. We will figure out the best course of action."

"I feel sorry for him." Laughlin looked surprised. "It's just I really got that he is sad, maybe whatever he learned recently was too much, and it pushed him into doing something out of character."

"Perhaps, but that is still to be determined. In fact, I need to get down and hear how the interrogation is going. Are you okay to be alone?"

I nodded. He kissed me gently on the forehead and quietly closed the door when he left. It was the first time since becoming Suri that I didn't want to be alone.

Chapter 22

Laughlin

I reluctantly left Suri to soak and recover. For the first time since I met her, she seemed fragile. Although I loved all aspects of her character, fragile was not one that I liked about her. But like us all, whatever she was going through would pass, and I would be there to help her repair.

I squared my shoulders and took a deep breath before I entered my work office. Opening the door, I saw that my brother, his mother, Annie, and Henry sat on the couch. Across from them, sat Geoff and Eddy. Thor was standing close to Eddy, clearly observing, and learning interrogation tactics from him.

When I entered, the men looked up at me questioningly regarding Suri. I nodded my head, not wanting to share out loud with our audience. I grabbed a chair and sat across from the trio. I was fascinated by my brother. He looked more like our father than I did, and we held similarities. It was odd to think that I had a family.

I stuck out my hand towards Malcolm. He looked at it then at me, not trusting what he was seeing. "It's a pleasure to meet you, Malcolm Fitzwilliam. Imagine my surprise, when I learned I had a brother."

A small, reluctant smile lifted the corners of his stiff lips, softening his look and giving some light to his dark eyes.

"Laughlin," was all he said as he shook my hand.

"Don't be deceived, Johnny boy, he's the devil. The devil, I say." Annie, who had been a servant in my family home my entire life, had become completely unhinged. Malcolm gazed at her as if truly seeing it for the first time. A pang of regret passed before his eyes before he shuttered them once again.

"Perhaps we can talk alone, without your mother as an audience." He nodded his head, and I strode from the room, with my brother in tow. "Take a good look around, Malcolm. If this is truly what you want, you can have it."

Behind me, Malcolm gazed at everything we passed. It wasn't a huge castle, but it was strategically placed, and its value was higher than most, with its proximity to the city.

When we were in my regular office, we sat down, and I poured us each a scotch. "Tell me about yourself and what you know," I ordered.

"There is not much to tell," he said, taking a big swig of his drink. "I was raised well, better than most, and although I lacked a mother. As you know, Sir Henry has been widowed for years now. I was cared for and loved."

"How is it we never met? Surely, one of us would have recognized the resemblance."

He nodded his head in agreement. "I think so too. In fact, it was your father who tipped me off. I happened to be walking by the study one day, and Henry was talking to your father. Beside me, was a mirror on the wall. For some reason, I chose that moment to look, and I saw it, the resemblance."

"So, he'd kept the secret. I can only imagine my father, and he contrived to keep your true lineage a secret, but why? Your mother's ravings didn't make any sense to me, besides that she is a spurned woman, so she clearly wanted revenge."

He dropped his head, and when he raised it again, there was a pain in his eyes that even his resting face couldn't hide. "I am responsible for our father's death, Laughlin. I am sorry."

"Tell me what happened."

"I had met my mother for the first time about a week before our father's death. She told me the story of her and Robert and how she has been working on a plan to gain my rightful inheritance. Until very recently, I didn't know she was a maid here. When we met, she talked about her wild, passionate nights with my father. She said your mother had pushed her away and broke their love because of money, then got pregnant with you to spite her. Anyway, at that point, I'd said nothing to Sir Henry but carried on as usual."

"So, he was truly in the dark regarding your actions?"

John nodded. "My mother told me when our father was flying out of Edinburgh, and I decided to confront him and ask him why he gave me away. It only took a few minutes to realize that he wasn't flying out of Edinburgh Airport, and I followed him to Perth."

He sat back, and his head dropped again. I quickly came to realize that this was a sign of preparation for revealing the truth. My father had a similar motion, only his head rose at an angle, like he was examining the person he was speaking with.

"Well, then all hell broke loose. I cut him off before he could get out of his car. I saw his face when he realized who I was, and it went from surprise to anger in under a second. It made me wonder what he would have been like as a father. Temperamental, I assume?"

I couldn't help but laugh. Malcolm's earnestness hit me,

and for some reason, that one comment amongst all the craziness was just what I needed to let go of the tension that had been holding my shoulders rigid since I heard the news of Suri's disappearance. "He was, and I would love to tell you more, but it must wait for now."

John accepted that with a nod. "I got out of my car, and he got out of his and asked me what I wanted. I told him the truth. He laughed at me and said which one. I'm not sure quite what that meant. Then he told me I was a bastard and should have no complaints, because I had been so well looked after. Before I could ask more, another car came screeching up, and two men, both with their faces covered, started shooting, not at me, at him. I ducked down, and he whipped a gun out of his inner jacket pocket and started firing back. Then he yelled at the men, calling them fucking SOGS. I was trying to figure out how I could help, as I had no gun or weapon of any kind. I'm embarrassed to say that until recently, I haven't been in a fight, either. Then I heard the tires squeal away. I stood and saw our father on the ground bleeding out from a gunshot wound to the chest. I took off my shirt and tried to stop the bleeding, but I knew he was dying. He looked at me and said, "I'm sorry," before he died.

Malcolm stopped then went on. "I didn't know what to do, so I called my mother, the only person who knew what I'd been up to. How it went from there, I don't know."

"Well then, let me fill you in, brother. Our father's body was found three days later, in a dig site in Palestine."

"What? How?"

"I'm assuming the SOGS, but continue, we can figure that out later.

"After that, I told my mother I wanted nothing to do with any of it. But she insisted that we needed to be reinstated to our rightful place. I don't know why she keeps saying that."

Suddenly, something clicked in my brain. "I think I do." I grabbed my phone and dialed Thor. "Can you please escort Sir Henry to my office?" When Henry arrived, I asked him to sit down, and I poured him a scotch and refilled mine and Malcolm's as well.

"Henry, I have a crucial question for you. Was my father ever married to Malcolm's mother?" Malcolm's eyes rounded with the question, but he turned his gaze to Henry, awaiting his answer.

Henry shifted uncomfortably and downed his scotch. "Yes, he was. When he was young and stupid, he fell in love with the maid's young daughter Annie, and the two had a passionate love affair. But Robert Sr. found out about it and had both women removed from employment. Annie and Robert continued to see each other in secret. When he found out she was pregnant, Robert wed her. When his father found out, he had it annulled and brought Annie back to the house to live through her pregnancy in comfort. The idea had been to give the baby up for adoption. But a few weeks later, Annie lost the baby. With Annie out of the way, Robert was then engaged to your mother, Laughlin, a Templar heiress. They became friends, but they never had the passion that he had with Malcolm's mother. Annie seemed to accept the new woman in Robert's life and their marriage and asked to stay on. Robert senior died not long after, and with no more obstacles, Robert went back to having an affair with Annie. Your mother didn't mind, Laughlin, as she looked at Annie as doing her a favor. Anyway, both women were pregnant, and Robert had to make a decision. He couldn't accept Annie's baby as his heir because of his marriage to Edith. So instead, he asked Marion and me to claim the baby as our own. As Marion couldn't have children, we looked at this as a win-win. The baby would be well looked after, loved, and within reach so Robert could see him from time to time.

The trouble started when Robert took Malcolm away from Annie right after birthing him, saying he was stillborn and quickly delivering him to me where I already had a nursemaid installed. No one was the wiser, and who would believe Annie, who somehow knew that Robert was lying to her? She seemed to deteriorate after that and, still, Robert loved her.

A few years later, Edith passed away from poisoning." He stopped and looked at me. "She never killed herself or died in childbirth. It was never proven, but Robert thought it was Annie who had poisoned her mistress. You found her, Laughlin. That is the suppressed memory you asked me about. Wracked with guilt, Robert never touched Annie again, and she became, as she appears today, a maid. Robert focused all of his attention on Laughlin, but not in the loving way that you had, Malcolm. Robert was entirely devoid of love after that had transpired. Laughlin, here, grew up without the love you had."

I don't know who was in more shock, my brother or myself.

"So, why does Annie think that she and Malcolm need to be restored?"

Henry sighed. "I think her memory has decided on a different story. She is the wife, and Edith is the seductress maid. Annie has been waiting all of this time to be restored to Robert's side as his rightful wife. Honestly, I think she lost her wits a long time ago. I told Robert that bad things would happen if he kept her here. But he felt responsible for her mental state."

"We should get her help. I will make some calls and get her into a facility, where she can be cared for and hopefully make a recovery. Is that okay with you, Malcolm?"

He seemed surprised that I asked for his opinion. "Yes, thank you, Laughlin. You are more than generous."

"No, but I will make things right between us. Henry, you

will give me your sworn testimony on Malcolm's character. Before meeting his mother, has he ever shown that he suffers from mental issues, sociopathic behavior, or a lack of conscience?"

"I swear on my life, Laughlin, Malcolm is a good man and has never committed a crime, nor been arrested for one. He has never been anything but kind and has a willing spirit. You two are only months apart and should be friends. For all intents and purposes, you are my son, Malcolm Robert Fitzwilliam, and will inherit my fortune and title when I die. If you are going to dispute Laughlin's claim to his inheritance, which you may, of course, it is going to get ugly. I think you two have a lot to discuss."

"We do," I said, looking at Malcolm, "but not tonight. Suri requires my presence. She is a little shaken up."

"I'm sorry, Laughlin, truly. I should have put an end to this, but my mother was quite convincing."

"I get it. Annie had worked here since before I was born, and I never guessed anything was amiss. We need to get Annie to a facility and set her up. Then, if you are agreeable, Malcolm, we can discuss the future. I will put in a call to a colleague and meet you both back in the other office."

After they left, I poured another scotch and texted Alice. Despite the hour, she answered me right away and put in a call to a top-notch facility run by a colleague she trusted. An hour later, Annie was escorted out of my home to her new one.

After making plans for the next day, I walked heavily up the stairs to my suite. Not everything was solved. There were still unanswered questions, but I was exhausted, and all I wanted was Suri. I found her asleep in my bed and watched for a moment as the moonlight splashed across her beautiful face, giving her that ethereal quality I loved.

Suri has many meanings, depending on the country of its origin. But my Suri's name derived from India and meant goddess. She was a goddess, and highlighted by the moon's glow, she was aptly named the moon goddess by me.

I slid into bed and pulled her close. She mumbled my name. "Aye, lass, it is me. All is well. Sleep, for tomorrow is a new beginning.

The End

Skylar West

Skylar West is a Canadian writer, new on the author scene and making a big impact with her steamy romance books. She loves walks in the rain, hot cups of delicious java, overly large sweaters, and the type of steamy sex she writes about in her novels. A cat lover, this author looks forward to writing many more novels.

Find her on Facebook: https://www.facebook.com/sky.west.1806

Don't miss these exciting titles by Skylar West and Blushing Books!

Crown and Cross series
Laughlin

Angels and Demons Series
Fallen Angel
Dark Angel Discovered
Dark Angel Awakened
Dark Angel Rescued
Dark Angel Redeemed

Single Titles
Marked
The Dark Side of Kingsley

Anthologies
12 Naughty Days of Christmas 2020

Blushing Books

Blushing Books is the oldest eBook publisher on the web. We've been running websites that publish steamy romance and erotica since 1999, and we have been selling eBooks since 2003. We have free and promotional offerings that change weekly, so please do visit us at http://www.blushingbooks.com/free.

Blushing Books Newsletter

Please join the Blushing Books newsletter
to receive updates & special promotional offers.
You can also join by using your mobile phone:
Just text **BLUSHING** to 22828.

Every month, one new sign up via text messaging will receive
a $25.00 Amazon gift card, so sign up today!